THE INNOCENT BONES

CHARMAINE STEWART

This is a work of fiction. Names, characters, businesses, places, events and incidents are either the products of the author's imagination or used in a fictitious manner. Any resemblance to actual persons, living or dead, or actual events is purely coincidental.

© Charmaine Stewart

First published in 2014
Cover models: Shanton Katire, Pelinawa Sakeus
Models by Louis Maruwasa/Agencia Models: agenciamodels@yahoo.com

Published by
Wordweaver Publishing House
P.O. Box 11579
Klein Windhoek
Windhoek, Namibia
info@wordweaverpublishing.com / www.wordweaverpublishing.com

ISBN 978-99945-82-00-6

Prologue

2010

"First, for the record Mma, what is your name?"

"Anna, Anna Nyembe."

"And how old are you?"

"At the beginning of the winter, I will be sixty-one years old."

"And where do you live?"

"In the location, here in Standerton."

"Your address, Mma."

"129 Geelhout Street."

"That's good. Now we can begin. Now, just in your own words, Mma..." Detective Jack Malepo held Mma Nyembe's hands gently, trying to calm her obvious distress. "No one is accusing you of anything. We just want to know what happened."

Mma Nyembe sniffed, straightened her tired back a little and said, almost to herself, "My own words. Yes, it is time to tell this story, time to bring it all into the light."

She lifted her gaze for the first time and looked the policeman directly in the eyes. "I am ready," she said. "I am ready to tell this terrible story. It has been a burden to me for most of my life."

She looked at the palms of her hands for a few moments, as if searching there for a place to start.

"It began in 1964, when I was still a very young woman.. That was the year I found a job working as a cleaner at the farm school about fifteen kilometres outside Standerton. It was a good job, and I was earning eight shillings every month. That doesn't sound much these days, but for me it was a lot of money. I sent most of the money I earned home to my mother and my sisters who lived on the farm in Lothair. I loved that job, and the children were like my children. I used to sit in the classroom while they were learning, and learned with them. I especially liked the sums, and practised doing them when the children were not watching. I stayed with my mother's brother and his wife."

She shook her head sadly. "He was a bad man, a wicked man who... he attacked me sometimes when my auntie was not there, and in a few months I found out I was pregnant."

1

She stopped for a few moments, remembering, and Detective Malepo remained completely silent, watching sadly, waiting for her to continue.

"I did not want my mother and my sisters to know of my shame, and also Mma Josie, the teacher. I did not want her to know I was pregnant. I was frightened that she would say I was a bad woman who should not be with children. So I kept it here," she held her closed fist to her chest, "a secret."

She fell silent for a while as Malepo watched silently. Then she began again.

"Maybe you think that my shame has nothing to do with this story, but in a way, that is what saved my life.

"It was just two weeks before Christmas and Mma Josie decided to take the children into the location in Standerton to see a film. It was a film about a white child who gets lost in the jungle and the gorillas look after him. I can't remember what it was called. The children loved the film, and as we walked back the fifteen kilometres to the school they were talking about it and pretending to be that white child, swinging through the trees.

"It was a very hot day, and the walk was long. The children were very hot. We were all hot, and when Mma Josie saw the vlei on the farm, she went to the farmer's wife and asked her if the children could swim in it. The farmer's wife said they could. They were all very happy and were soon splashing in the water running over the rocks. Even Mma Josie and Mma Elsie took off their shoes and cooled their feet in the water."

Anna Nyembe seemed to have gone back to her youth, even sounding younger.

"Because I was pregnant, I needed the toilet too often, and we were far from a toilet. So I went behind the big trees next to the vlei and hid from everyone while I relieved myself. Suddenly, I heard a vehicle drive up and a man started shouting at Mma Josie and the children. I was frightened. I looked out between the branches of the tree and saw a white policeman and a Black Maria. You know the Black Maria?"

"I know, Mma," Detective Malepo said gently. The sight of a black police van with this frightening name was enough to strike terror into most black people's hearts in the bad days. Anyone without a pass to be in a certain area was rounded up like a stray dog. The lucky ones were beaten and returned to where they came from. Not everyone was lucky in those days. Not everyone went home.

Mma Nyembe looked up from her tightly clenched hands, straight into Jack Malepo's eyes.

"I saw him as I see you now. He was a policeman. I saw his uniform."

She looked to see if Malepo believed her. Reassured that he did, she smiled gratefully and asked if there was some water as her throat was getting dry. She said she was not used to talking so much.

Malepo brought her some water but knew the request for what it was. She was afraid to go on with her story, afraid of what would result from breaking her silence after forty years.

He handed her the glass, which she accepted from his hands in the traditional African way, her left hand cradling her right wrist.

"Go on, Mma," he said gently, "you are doing very well."

The old lady took a few sips from the glass and placed it gently on the table before her. Then she covered her eyes with her hand for a few moments. Detective Malepo waited patiently.

The next part was the hardest. Anna Nyembe had carried the shame of her betrayal within her breast for nearly half a century. She was about to reveal it for the first time.

"He was shouting that the children were dirtying the water that the cows drink from. Then he took a big knobkierrie out of his van and he hit those children like dogs, chasing them out of the water. The children were crying. Mma Josie ran to stop him. She shouted that the farmer's wife had said that the children could swim. He turned and called her a liar, and he called her many bad names. Then he hit her very hard in her face and she fell. Her head hit the rocks on the side of the vlei. She did not move. I was so frightened. I thought maybe she was dead. The children and Mma Elsie were very quiet, but then the little ones started to cry again."

The tears coursed down Anna's cheeks and were brushed away by thin arthritic hands.

"I stood there," she murmured, "I just stood there while he held a gun and told Mma Elsie and the children to climb into the Black Maria. Then he picked up Mma Josie and threw her in too, as if she was a sack of mealies. I just stood. I did nothing to stop him. And then he drove them away, leaving me standing there still, hiding like a thief between the willow trees."

She held her jersey to her face to hide her shame, the tears streaming down her cheeks.

Malepo put a hand on her shoulder to comfort her.

"What do you think you could have done, Mma," he asked gently, "hardly more than a child yourself, alone and pregnant? Did you see any of them again?"

"No," she whispered. "I never saw them again. One day we had a school with a teacher and children, and the next day there was an empty building."

"Did the parents not come looking for their children? Did they not report the disappearance to the police?"

She shook her head, her misery and shame etched deep into her lined face.

"I don't know. I didn't stay there to find out. I was frightened that the policeman would come and find me. I went home to my mother and told her my shame, told her of the child I was carrying and about my bad uncle. But I never told this story to another person, never... until today."

Jack Malepo rocked back in his seat, riveted by what he had heard, and astounded that he could find no record of the missing women and children.

Even in those terrible days, surely the disappearance of seven children, a young woman and a teacher would have resulted in an investigation? Parents would have searched for their children. Missing person's reports would have been filed. Enquiries would have been made. Surely!

He needed to dig further. There was absolutely nothing on file in the official police records. It was as if the disappearance of all these people had occurred without comment from anyone – parents, relatives, police or community. If it was not for the physical evidence, he would think that the story was the result of an old woman's overactive imagination.

"Mma, I want you to do something for me. I want you to come back and tell me the whole story. But I don't want you to talk to anyone else about this. I know it was a long time ago, but evil hangs over this story, and evil has a way of repeating itself."

Chapter 1

1929

Hennie's first memory of Jakkalsvlei was standing beside his mother's grave in a small fenced area dotted with gravestones and surrounded by tall dusty cypress trees. The heat was intense, forming mirages of phantom lakes across the dry fields that faded towards the distant blue mountains. The hypnotic sound of the dominee's voice was drowned out by the sound of dry red soil being shovelled on top of his mother's coffin by two black farm workers, their bare backs glistening with sweat.

The sound of the soil landing on the thin wooden coffin was the most awful sound of Hennie's young life, and one which would remain with him for many years.

His father's rough skin was comforting as he held Hennie's small hand. When the dominee finished his prayer, his father squeezed his hand and led him gently away from the graveside. He took Hennie over to the sombre-looking family who were standing across the grave from them.

Hennie's father nodded to his brother-in-law, who nodded back. No words were spoken by either man. His father then pushed Hennie firmly but gently towards this forbidding stranger, turned around, and walked away. Hennie watched in consternation as his father mounted his horse. An impulse to follow was curbed by a hard hand gripping his shoulder.

His father wheeled the horse around in a cloud of fine dust, and man and horse gradually disappeared into the shimmering midday heat. Hennie never saw his father again. He never said goodbye and he never returned.

The small bundle with his few possessions lay in the dust along the path to the farmhouse. A boy some years older than Hennie picked it up easily and slung it over his shoulder. He shot a sympathetic look over at his small cousin, gave him a quick grin, and with a jerk of his head indicated that Hennie should follow. Hennie's heart lightened a little. He needed a friend, and who better than this sturdy blonde boy. He followed at his cousin's heels like a small dog, the start of half a lifetime of devotion.

Once the dominee's cart had disappeared in the direction of Standerton, the rest of the family followed the boys to the house. Hennie was very aware of his stern uncle and soft plump aunt. The presence of a quiet little girl about his own age barely registered with him.

The house consisted of two rooms, a living room and a sleeping room, surrounded on all sides by a covered stoep which was accessed from the north by three worn steps. A corrugated iron roof covered the house, rusted to a colour not too different from the red earth on which the house stood. There was a shack to one side where the cooking was done. Nearby, a hand pump with a metal bucket supplied water for drinking and washing. An outhouse, or kleinhuisie, stood some distance from the house, down a path edged with small rocks and a few straggling plants, overhung by a huge acacia tree. A skeletal yellow-eyed dog sniffed Hennie suspiciously and then ambled into the yard, where he flopped down in the meagre shade of a camel thorn tree.

In the distance, Hennie could see the vlei that gave Jakkalsvlei its name. It looked cool and inviting, hung with bright green willows. He would have loved to shed his clothes and jump into its cool freshness, but the blonde boy nudged him in the direction of the stoep, where he dropped Hennie's bundle. He left, returning a few minutes later with a small metal trunk containing a roll-up mattress and a thin blanket.

"I am Cobus, your cousin. You'll be sleeping here on the stoep with me," he said. "Now, put your things into the trunk, and come with me. There is work to be done."

Chapter 2

2010

Thuli sat on the narrow bench trying to drown out the chatter of the crowd, clutching the paddle firmly in her hand. She knew the lot number, had checked out the property, and was determined to win her house. This was the first auction she had ever attended, and her excitement battled with her nervousness.

It seemed to take forever for Lot 127 to come up. Surreptitiously, she watched as the properties came and went. She made a note of the way others were bidding, and who was successful in the bidding for the various properties. She knew that she must not seem too eager, but it took every scrap of her willpower not to lift her paddle the moment the auctioneer's assistant called her lot number.

Suddenly, the crowd seemed to disappear and the noise became a distant hum. All her attention was focused on the auctioneer standing at the front of the room.

She waited, not daring to breathe as he called the opening bid... once... then twice. She lifted her paddle slowly but resolutely, as if this was not the culmination of many years of constant work and sacrifice coming to fruition.

"Damn," Thuli thought as the auctioneer acknowledged a second bidder. She recognised the man as a local property developer. She hoped that he had set himself a limit, one well short of hers. She nodded her bid emphatically as the auctioneer looked at her again. She was well within the maximum she had agreed with herself. As the bidding progressed, she prayed that the property developer would lose interest. As the price nudged higher and higher, closer to her limit, a feeling of panic spread through her. She felt perspiration trickle down her back, a clear indication that her stress levels were sky-high.

"Please God, give me this one!" she prayed. At the same time, she crossed her fingers and ankles and held her thumbs, hedging her bets.

Just as the bidding reached to within five thousand rand of her limit, the developer faltered and then gave up, shaking his head regretfully. Thuli had to prevent herself from dancing with joy as the auctioneer's gavel hit the desk. Soon she was finalising the details with the clerk, trying to look cool and confident, as if this was something she did every day.

As she left the auction room about an hour later in a state of wild exhilaration, the first person she phoned was her grandmother.

"I've got it, Gogo!" she shouted as she heard her grandmother's voice.

"If that is what you truly want, my child, then I'm happy for you," replied her grandmother gravely, "but I have a bad feeling about this. I think you are getting yourself in deeper than you think. Besides, you know that I'm happy for you to live here with me forever."

"I know that, Gogo," replied Thuli gently, "but I am twenty-seven years old, and it is time I started standing on my own feet. I can't rely on you forever. You have been better than a mother to me since I was a baby, and I owe you everything. But I need to do this. Please don't be hurt! I love you so much."

"Aish, be quiet child," laughed her grandmother. "You know I can never say no to you. Just be careful, and know that you will always have a place here with me. You're my family."

"I'll be there every Sunday for lunch, you won't be losing your granddaughter," smiled Thuli. Then she suddenly exclaimed, "Darn! I'm late getting back to the bank. They'll be wondering what I've been doing."

"You get back then," laughed her grandmother. "You don't want to lose your good job so soon after your promotion."

"You're right about that! Bye, Gogo, see you tonight!"

Thuli smiled to herself as she crossed the road, hugging her secret to herself. She had told no one at the bank that she was buying a house, least of all in an affluent, formerly white area.

She was a very private person with a single-minded determination and a reputation for being a hard worker. She was on friendly terms with all her colleagues but had not made any close friends at the bank. She started as Junior Manager and had recently been promoted to Commercial Manager. Although her promotion did not surprise anyone but Thuli herself, she quickly took to her new role. She had been at the bank for three years now, and had received an excellent evaluation just three weeks earlier.

Thuli had been one of the brightest students in her class at university, the one most people thought would go far. Once she had her MBA degree, she confounded her friends and lecturers at university by returning to the rural backwater of Standerton. She did not explain that she wanted to stay close to her only family – her grandmother – who had raised her since she was born, when her mother had died of AIDS. She knew that one day she might want to move back to the city, but not while her grandmother was still alive.

Gogo, believing that education was the passport to a better life, had made tremendous sacrifices to ensure that Thuli was well educated. She had worked with Thuli in the afternoons as she studied, insisting that this was giving her the opportunity that she herself had not had as a child. Gogo had only attended school until she was twelve years old. A black girl child was required to take up the responsibilities of the household early in those days, and hours spent at school were considered hours wasted.

Thuli had not disappointed her. While other girls were dreaming about clothes and boys, Thuli had spent hours studying, working towards the bursary which was her entry into university. Although Gogo was quite willing to pay for her university education, Thuli was determined to stand on her own feet financially. She wished to make Gogo feel proud, that the sacrifices she had made bringing up her only granddaughter had been worth it.

Chapter 3

Thuli made many friends at school but her best friend was Katie van Tonder. Although they were different in every possible way, they became friends during their first year of school and remained inseparable all their lives.

Katie had a serious problem with spelling and writing. Thuli spent hours with her every afternoon, trying to teach her. The two little girls cried every afternoon as Katie tried to spell the words that Thuli found so easy, and they cried when Katie was humiliated by her teachers for being stupid and failing her spelling tests.

Katie was twelve before her mother, Julie, finally convinced her father that their daughter needed some help. A visit to a child psychologist confirmed what her mother had always known – that Katie was extremely intelligent. She also told Julie that Katie had dyslexia.

Katie was relieved to know that her teachers were wrong about her. She was not stupid at all. Instead, she had a learning difficulty over which she had no control. While this helped her to overcome some of her complexes, it did not help her academically. Nor did it stop the bullying by some pupils, or change the attitude of her teachers, who still considered her stupid and unteachable.

By the time she was sixteen, Katie had had enough. The school year had ended with another damning report card. She watched her parents' faces as they read the report; her mother's sympathy, her father's disappointment. Her moment had arrived.

"I am not going back to school next year," she said firmly but quietly. She was not confrontational, simply stating a fact.

"Don't be ridiculous!" snapped her father, Rick. "You will complete your schooling. Then we can decide what we will do with you. You are a pretty little thing, you will soon find a husband and have a litter of children."

"I don't want to be just another housewife. No insult intended to you, Mom, but this is a different world. Women have careers. I want a career. I want to be a photographer."

"Photography isn't a career, it's a hobby! Besides, women don't have careers. They have husbands to take care of them. Look at your mother, she is very happy being a housewife. She wouldn't have wanted to continue as a nurse after you were born, would you have, Julie?"

Julie muttered something inaudible and stood up to take the dishes through to the kitchen.

Katie persevered with her arguments, which continued through December and into January. The new school year was looming, and with it the potential end to Katie's dreams. But every time she brought up her plans, Rick would put her off. Eventually, he banned the subject altogether and refused to discuss it, either shutting Katie up or storming out of the house in protest.

"These things are best left to people who are more experienced in the ways of the world than you, people who have your best interests at heart. One day you will thank me for being firm," her father said loftily.

He was relieved when Katie appeared to give up, satisfied that her little rebellion was thoroughly squashed. But he relaxed his vigilance too soon.

Rick had not bargained on his mousy and obedient wife joining Katie's rebellion. Julie contacted an old school friend, Angela Markus, who had long before confounded the sceptics and made a name for herself as a gifted photographer. Soon the plot was hatched. Three days before the start of the school term, Katie boarded a shuttle to Johannesburg with a suitcase full of clothes, her old Nikon camera, and a bank account with a small inheritance from her grandmother to cover her immediate expenses.

Julie waved until the Volkswagen shuttle had disappeared over the bridge. The tears in her eyes were happy tears. She hoped Katie might have the opportunities she herself had missed. Drying her eyes, she headed back home to break the news to Rick. She had never been a brave or confident person, but in defence of her daughter she had the courage of a lioness.

Angela Markus was a formidable and highly skilled woman, not only as a photographer but also as a teacher. She hid a warm and motherly instinct behind a stern façade that seldom fooled anyone.

A large lady, she dressed in multiple layers and bright colours. The effect was a plump bird of paradise. Angela insisted that Katie live in her home, surrounded by her boisterous family and a menagerie of dogs, cats and a very bad-tempered parrot.

Katie soon became one of the family. She worked harder than she had ever worked before, revelling in the demanding tasks and challenges. While her friends were out enjoying themselves over the weekends, Katie was carrying heavy camera cases, working under hot spotlights, and spending long hours in the darkroom.

For the first time in her life, Katie was doing what she loved. At last she was involved in something that did not require her to spell or write. It brought out the best in her, and she became more confident and outgoing.

Katie adored Angela and her family, and blossomed under the uncritical affection they showered on her.

At the end of her three-year apprenticeship, it was time for her to move into the real world. With an excellent portfolio built up during her years with Angela, Katie was able to secure a position as resident photographer with a large clothing chain. The change was made easier when she found a cottage half an hour's drive from Angela's house, where Katie knew she could always expect a daughter's welcome.

Although she enjoyed the work and the independence, it was Katie's ambition to be a freelance fashion photographer, able to pick and choose her jobs. She worked non-stop developing her portfolio, and circulated it to the larger magazine publishers in South Africa. Breaking into the fashion market was not easy. It took about a year, but eventually Katie started getting the occasional contract. Every time she saw one of her photographs in print, she felt the thrill of ownership.

Only the very gifted and fortunate make it in the glamorous world of fashion. But the combination of her natural good looks and her uncanny ability to frame the perfect shot helped Katie to make a breakthrough. By the time she was twenty-five, she was doing photo shoots for glossies around the world. The name Katie van Tonder was suddenly on everyone's lips.

When Thuli decided to move back to Standerton at the end of her studies, Katie was disappointed, though she understood and sympathised with Thuli's reasons. Suddenly, meeting up was a two-hour trip either way for one of them, and with Katie's travel commitments, these trips became fewer and fewer. Even the telephone calls began to taper off, and Thuli found that she was really missing her old friend.

Chapter 4

As the ambulance stopped and its doors opened to reveal the front door of the Woodlands Retirement Home, Van Tonder realised that something was seriously wrong. He was expecting to be dropped back at his home and was looking forward to getting back to his normal routine. The wheelchair would be a hindrance but he was confident that, despite his eighty-eight years and a recently broken pelvis, he would be well able to take care of himself. After two weeks spent in hospital and then another month in the convalescent wing trying without success to become fully mobile again, he was longing to be back in the peace and quiet of his own home.

The ambulance men quickly pulled out the stretcher and tried to help him into the chair that was wheeled out by a plump woman in a white uniform and a gleaming smile.

"What are you doing?" he demanded in a panicky voice, looking up at the imposing entrance of the building. "I'm not staying here. You've made a mistake. You should have taken me home. I should be at home!"

Neither of the ambulance men replied, too used to this sort of situation to want to get involved.

"Hey! I'm talking to you!" shouted Van Tonder frantically, fighting them off and trying to get out of the chair, his corset hampering his movements.

"Come along now, Mr van Tonder," said the nurse in the sort of voice one uses with a child. "We are expecting you and have a lovely room ready for you."

"This is a mistake," he insisted. "I don't want your lovely room. I have my own house and I'm going back there. Tell them to take me back to my house."

"No, there is no mistake," replied the nurse kindly. "You'll be staying here from now on. I am sure you will settle quickly and be very happy here."

"Where's my son?" shouted Van Tonder, becoming more distressed by the moment, hitting out feebly at the ambulance men and succeeding in landing a weak blow.

"That sort of behaviour isn't tolerated here, Mr van Tonder," said the nurse firmly. Van Tonder felt a sharp prick in his arm as strong arms strapped him into the chair.

He was aware of being wheeled along a long corridor to a private suite, where he was changed into pyjamas and helped into bed. He watched in a haze as his small bag was unpacked into cupboards which already contained

13

many of his possessions; things he had left in his own home only six weeks previously.

He was completely disorientated, as if he was suddenly living someone else's life. He felt helpless, powerless and very frightened.

Van Tonder spent the first two days at the home fruitlessly demanding to see his son, and then less confidently pleading to see the manager. On the third day, he succeeded in getting the nurses to arrange a meeting with the matron.

"I am Matron Marjorie, Mr van Tonder," she said as she came into his room. "I understand you have been asking to see me."

Van Tonder eyed her with displeasure for a few moments, irritated that the person in charge was a woman, and a black woman at that. Realising that there was no alternative, he resigned himself to the fact that he would have to deal with her, unsatisfactory as that was for him.

"I need to see my son," he said. "Someone has made a mistake. I didn't ask to be brought here, and no one seems to be able to sort out this mess. I need to speak to my son to sort out the problem."

"There is no problem, Mr van Tonder," she replied patiently. "It was your son who booked you in here. You are now a permanent guest and will remain with us from now on."

"That is impossible!" Van Tonder shouted, tearful and furious. "I never agreed to come here and I'm certainly not staying. No one has any right to keep me here against my will. I want to go home."

"That is not possible, I'm afraid," Matron Marjorie answered, shaking her head sympathetically. "However, I'll telephone your son and ask him to come and see you when he has time."

With that small concession, Van Tonder had to be satisfied.

Chapter 5

Thuli was busy packing. She was very methodical, carefully numbering and categorising each box. Several boxes stood around her room, some empty, some half packed, some sealed and ready to go.

She heard the sound of the doorbell, and then her grandmother talking to someone. Suddenly, Thuli heard a familiar voice and flew to the front door.

It was Katie, arriving out of the blue and flashing an engagement ring.

"So, what do you think?" she asked nervously.

"Oh my god, it's enormous!" shrieked Thuli. "Did you get that rock in a lucky packet, or as a bauble at some fashion shoot?"

"No, silly – this is an engagement ring," laughed Katie, with mock condescension. "If you'd paid more attention to boys rather than your books when we were growing up, you would know about these things."

"Engagement ring," Thuli laughed, arching her eyebrows at her best friend. "So, who are you engaged to? The last I heard you were playing off a Spanish property developer against an English banker."

"Playing is right. Just games," scoffed Katie. "Besides, that was about two years ago. This is serious."

"I've heard that before, but somehow this time I believe you. Who is it? Do I know him?"

"Yes, you do," said Katie.

"Oh?" replied Thuli, mystified. This was a surprise to her as, due to their very different careers, she and Katie did not share many friends.

Katie seemed a little coy about revealing the identity of her fiancé.

"Come on. Don't keep me in suspense," demanded Thuli. "Tell me."

"Do you remember Patrick Tshabalala?"

"Of course I remember him," Thuli gasped. "Don't tell me you're marrying Patrick?"

Katie nodded, beaming happily.

"Wow! How on earth did you meet up with him again? And where? He moves in such elite circles these days. The only time I ever hear about him is on the sports news or in the glossies, and occasionally when I happen to see the sports pages in the papers. He is still a big hero in South Africa, and especially here in Standerton, one of the best footballers of his generation, according to the papers. He has certainly come a long way from being captain of the school football team."

Suddenly she stopped, a look of horror on her face.

"Have you spoken to your father? What does he say about you marrying a black man?"

If it was not for Katie's mother, Julie, Rick van Tonder's prejudice would have meant an early death to the friendship between the girls. Julie was not a forceful person, but she believed that Thuli was a good influence on Katie and stood her ground regarding their friendship. But that did not mean her father did not make his feelings abundantly clear to his family, and to those he held in such contempt.

When Katie's father was present, Thuli was left in no doubt that she was an unwelcome guest in his home. She knew that Rick would be furious and totally opposed to the marriage, and worried that her friend would have hard times ahead.

"I have not had the courage to tell him." Katie looked ashamed. "When I saw Patrick again after all these years, I just fell in love with him all over again. We knew this time it was right. We aren't children anymore, and this time my father was not there to put a spanner in the works."

Like Katie, Patrick had battled with dyslexia, and this had formed a bond between them, even though Patrick was three years ahead of her at school.

Besides being a sweet-natured and gentle soul, Patrick had one outstanding talent – his ability to kick a football. At the age of fourteen he was already the school's top footballer, and by the time he left, he had been football captain for an unprecedented three years running. The word soon spread that there was an extraordinary talent in this rural backwater, and several top clubs expressed an interest in signing him.

Patrick's mother, Eva, was fiercely ambitious for her only son but she wanted him to complete his schooling before being swallowed up by the world of football. She dealt cannily with the talent scouts, keeping them keen to sign but patient enough to wait.

Katie was at every football game, his loudest and most loyal supporter.

While mixed-race relationships in the cities were becoming more and more acceptable, the old prejudices still lived on in the country towns, especially with people like Rick van Tonder.

He was determined to break up the friendship forming between his pretty blonde daughter and the school's black football star. In the face of Katie's obstinate refusal to stop seeing Patrick, he dealt with the threat in typical fashion.

He chose his moment carefully, waiting until he and his father were standing around the braai in the garden, beers in hand, while the women prepared salads in the kitchen.

"I need a favour, Pa," Rick said.

"What is it?" asked the older Van Tonder.

"It's Katie. She has been getting a little too interested in a boy at school, and I need some help to break it up."

"Already! She is only thirteen years old. Do we know the boy?" his father asked.

"It's a black boy from the location," answered Rick with distaste, mortified that his daughter had put him in such a difficult position.

"Is he from a good family?"

"No!" lied Rick. "Just some skollie from the wrong side of the tracks."

His father was horrified. His only granddaughter hanging around with someone like that! It was not something he had ever thought possible.

"Well, we can't have that," he spluttered. "I thought the girl had sense. I still have a few friends who owe me some favours. Talk to Pieter Bruyns, he will soon sort the fucker out."

It was a simple matter for Van Tonder to put his plan into action.

Three days later, as Patrick left football practice, he was stopped by two cops who ordered him into the police car. Mystified but obedient, Patrick complied, but within a few minutes he wished he had rather made a run for it.

Although it was just a five-minute drive from the school to the police station, it was several hours before they arrived at their destination. Patrick's mother was there, waiting. It was a small town and she had known within minutes that her son had been picked up by the cops. The sight of her son awoke the lioness in her. Patrick was in a daze; handcuffed, beaten and bloody.

After what seemed like a very long night in a cell he appeared before the magistrate, charged with drug dealing. A bag of marijuana was produced which the cops claimed to have found in his sports bag. A charge of resisting arrest was thrown in for good measure. Three police officers testified to his violent and aggressive behaviour. Based on their evidence, Patrick was remanded in custody and denied bail. Confused and frightened, he pleaded to be allowed to go home, but to no avail.

The instinct of a mother to protect her young is one of the strongest forces on earth, and when Eva Tshabalala saw her son come into the police station all bloodied, she came out fighting. She was not going to allow her only son to sit in prison for another night. As she left the courtroom, she was on the line to the talent scout from Orlando Pirates, who had been following

Patrick's progress. In exchange for getting Patrick out of the cell unscathed and without a criminal record, she was willing to make a deal, which was that Patrick would go to Johannesburg immediately and start training for Pirates.

Alvin Klatzow, a sharp lawyer representing Orlando Pirates, arrived from Johannesburg just too late to represent Patrick in court. That did not bother him. He was familiar with the way things worked and quickly did some negotiating of his own. Neither Patrick nor Eva knew how he achieved it, but before nightfall the charges were dropped and Patrick was free to leave.

In a way, though, Rick had succeeded in his plan because, within twenty-four hours of his arrest, Patrick Tshabalala had left Standerton and disappeared out of Katie's life, as far as he knew, forever.

Rick was very pleased with the result of his intervention but was to pay a huge price – the loss of his daughter's love and trust.

Katie was devastated at Patrick's disappearance and wept hot tears into her pillow every night for months. She was sure that both her father and grandfather had been involved in his arrest and subsequent departure, and her already strained relationship with the two of them deteriorated. Katie refused to visit her grandfather, and when he came to their house she would remain in her room, or go out.

For a while, Patrick seemed to disappear into thin air. Nobody knew where he was or what had happened to him. It was six months later when Katie heard his name again, in the school yard. It appeared that Patrick was making his name as a rising star for Orlando Pirates. Katie spent hours reading the sport pages, looking for his name and watching his progress. She longed for him to contact her. Eventually, she had to accept that he had forgotten her and that they would never be together.

Two years later, the papers reported that Patrick had left Orlando Pirates for Chelsea and the English football scene. Soon he was making a name for himself on the green football fields of England. He couldn't have seemed further away if he had been on the moon.

And now this! Thuli felt as if she was in a dream.

"How on earth did you meet up with him again, after all these years? What's he like? Has he changed?"

"Well, I was doing a photo shoot for GQ in London, and who should be the star of the shoot, but Patrick himself! As soon as I saw him, my heart was in my mouth. I didn't think he would remember me after all these years, but he did. He stood there like a statue and just kept saying "Katie, Katie" over and over. It was as if we had both been struck by lightning. I could barely control my camera I was shaking so much, especially since he was standing there in just his football shorts and looking so amazing."

18

Thuli laughed. "This is the craziest thing I've ever heard. So, when did this happen?"

Katie pulled a face. "Three months ago," she said with a nervous smile. "Is this too fast? Do you think I'm totally crazy? Tell me if you think I am. I know my father will hit the roof, and I really need your support, Thuli. Will you come with me to tell him? Please?"

Thuli laughed.

"You bet I will. I'm dying to see his face when he gets this news. Besides, I've other news to tell him. You know your grandfather's house was put on auction a few weeks ago? Well, guess who bought it? I take ownership at the end of the month."

"My grandfather's house? But you hate that house."

"Yes, and no. I always thought it was a beautiful house, despite what happened that day, so perhaps there was just a little element of revenge in my buying it."

"Well, that's poetic justice!" laughed Katie. "It serves Oupa right. I will never forgive him for the way he treated you when we were kids."

"Yes, I suppose there is some sort of poetic justice about it. I've been searching for a house for ages; something I could afford and turn into my dream home. And then I saw your grandfather's house was being offered on auction. My common sense told me I was being ridiculous, but in my heart I knew I had to have it. I was determined to live in the house that the old man had chucked me out of when I was just eight years old."

Chapter 6

Although Van Tonder was in no way resigned to his situation, he was getting used to the routine at Woodlands. Every morning, each resident had ten minutes in the bathroom before being collected and wheeled through to the dining room for breakfast. After breakfast, the residents were placed in a row in front of the television in the lounge. Looking at the vacant faces around him, Van Tonder assumed that the others were as bored by the reruns of ancient soap operas as he was.

Every Tuesday morning there was the weekly visit from the occupational therapist. On Wednesdays, a hairdresser would come to cut everyone's hair in an identical style, male or female, while on Fridays a mobile library would do the rounds, offering a small selection of books.

Once a week another therapist would come and do what he called chair gym, where everyone sat around in a circle and went through a series of seated exercises to the accompaniment of music. This was a surprisingly popular activity, and Van Tonder guessed that inside those shrivelled bodies there still remained a love of music and dance.

After a bland lunch, all the residents would be wheeled out to sit on the stoep overlooking the gardens until supper time. There was nothing to do, not even a game of Scrabble or a newspaper to challenge the mind.

Van Tonder had been at Woodlands for six weeks and was sitting on the stoep seething at his inability to get around and the pointlessness of his current lifestyle, when he saw Rick's car coming up the drive. If he could have leapt to his feet, he would have. Instead, he waited with barely controlled impatience for his son to come up the stairs to where he was sitting.

"It's about time you showed your face," he snarled when Rick had greeted him. "I've been sitting here for months. Where the hell have you been?"

"I am sorry, Pa," said Rick. "There have been a hundred things to do, and I didn't want to come until everything was sorted out."

"Well, thank God you have finally come to take me away!" he said, hiding his relief at seeing a familiar face behind an angry bluster. "That bloody matron tried to tell me that you had booked me in here for the rest of my life."

Rick picked up a chair and sat down facing his father, frowning at the papers he held in his hands. It had been a tough time for him. He dreaded breaking the news to his father, and the strain showed on his sweaty face and shaking hands.

"I'm afraid she's right, Pa," he said quietly. "You'll be staying here from now on."

"What? Have you taken leave of your fucking senses? I'll do no such thing!" roared his father. "You'll go and pack my bag right now and take me to my house."

He had every expectation of being obeyed. As gentle as he had been with Elmarie, he had brought up his son with a rod of iron, and still expected to be obeyed without question.

Rick looked at him, a mixture of contempt and pity on his face.

"Sorry, Pa," he said. "I'm afraid you don't give the orders anymore. I have been to the court and am now officially your guardian."

"My what?" yelled Van Tonder.

Rick ignored his outburst and continued in the words he had rehearsed all the way to Woodlands.

"That means I have complete authority over you and all your affairs, both personal and financial. You are not in a fit state to look after yourself anymore. I don't have the time to take care of you myself, so I have booked you in here where you will be well cared for. It's in your best interests."

"That is absolute bullshit and you know it," shouted his father. "I want to go home now, and if you won't take me, I will get a taxi and go by myself."

"Pa, you don't have a house anymore. It was sold on auction and the sale was finalised yesterday. Once the transfer has gone through the funds will be deposited into a trust account that I've set up for you."

Van Tonder gaped at his son, for once totally lost for words.

"I am sorry, Pa, but this place costs plenty. The money from the sale of the house will pay for your accommodation here until you die."

The blood drained from Van Tonder's face and when he finally found his voice, it came out in a croak.

"You'd like me to die, wouldn't you? I raised you and your sister, spent the best years of my life taking care of you, and this is how you treat me?"

Rick hung his head. He did not have an easy answer.

"You have no right to take my house. You need to go and tell them you've changed your mind. I have to get back to my house."

"It's too late. I couldn't even if I wanted to, and I don't want to," answered Rick, his face red, the strain of the conversation showing in his neck and hands. In spite of everything, he had never been able to stand up to his domineering father.

"Then I'm going to get hold of Douw Steyn and sue you for every penny you have. I'm going to sue you for kidnapping, fraud and theft. And then I'm going to get my house back, if it's the last thing I do."

"Pa, for goodness sake, Douw Steyn doesn't practise law anymore and hasn't done so for thirty years. He's had Alzheimer's for the past fifteen years."

"Rubbish, he's the best legal brain in the country," said Van Tonder, grappling desperately for some authority.

"He might have been once, Pa," said Rick impatiently, "but like you, he is now an old man who needs to have his nappy changed four times a day and be fed like a baby. I'm sorry, but I can't spend the rest of my life running around looking after you. This is the best solution, and one that will benefit both you and me."

He looked at his father, half with bitterness and half with sadness.

"If Elmarie or Ma were still alive it would be different. But as things go, it's only you and me, and I'm not willing or able to take on that responsibility."

Rick stood up and walked away, his father's curses following him all the way to his car. He sat in the car for a few minutes to calm his nerves, brushing away the tears that trickled unbidden down his cheeks. He desperately needed to get home; to get as far away from his father and Woodlands as he could. He felt strange and disoriented. When he looked at himself in the rear view mirror, his face seemed to him to be the face of a stranger, twisted and distorted.

Then Rick fell forward onto the steering wheel, oblivious to the drawn-out hooting of the car's horn.

Chapter 7

Two days after Katie's unexpected arrival at Thuli's door, the friends were sitting in Thuli's Audi outside Rick van Tonder's house, bracing themselves for the confrontation they were sure was to come. Katie took Thuli's hand and squeezed it. Then they got out of the car and started up the garden path towards the front door.

But before they had taken more than a few steps, Julie burst out of the house and came running down the path towards them, clearly distraught.

"Katie, my darling!" she cried. "Where have you been? I have been trying to contact you since yesterday."

"I have been staying with Thuli and her granny. Did you try my mobile?"

"I can never get used to those things," answered her mother crossly. "You really should let people know when you are going away. Besides, why are you staying with Thuli and not with us if you are in town?"

"Long story, Mum," answered Katie shortly. "Now, what was it that was so important?"

"It's your father," answered Julie. "He had a very bad stroke in his car outside the retirement home yesterday afternoon. He's in hospital. I wanted you to come home and see him ... and here you are." She smiled weakly with relief and triumph, as if she had personally solved a problem.

"A stroke? How bad is it?" asked Katie, giving her mother a strong hug.

"It seems very bad indeed," Julie said, shaking her head. "He is conscious but he can't move or talk. Oh my baby, I'm so happy you are home. Come! We must go to the hospital straight away."

"Thuli," Katie said, turning to her friend and holding both her hands, "you understand, don't you?"

"Of course," answered Thuli, with an enquiring look at her friend. "Katie, will you be okay?"

"I suppose we will have to postpone our news, yours and mine, until my father has recovered," Katie answered sadly.

"News, what news?" asked Julie.

"Nothing that can't wait, Mom," answered Katie affectionately.

The friends hugged each other. "I'll spend some time with my mom while my father's in hospital. I'll come and fetch my stuff later," said Katie.

"You take care," answered Thuli, "and don't give up your plans because of a temporary setback. You deserve to be happy."

Chapter 8

1929

Hennie's work that first day consisted of carrying the bucket with the feed for the chickens and watching as Cobus fed them. Once the chickens were fed, the boys carefully collected the eggs and took them to the cooking shack.

That first night was the most frightening of Hennie's young life. He was used to the town with its lights and noises and the sound of his father snoring in the next room. He was used to having a bed and a bedroom to sleep in, and a mother to kiss him goodnight.

At Jakkalsvlei, all he had was a battered metal trunk for his clothes, a roll-up mattress on the dusty floor of the stoep, and a thin blanket. The dark night sky and deep silence were broken only by terrifying and unfamiliar noises. Flying things swooped over his bed; night animals hooted, yelped and shrieked. This was a strange and frightening place. He cried that night and many nights after that, but secretly and silently so as not to shame himself in front of Cobus.

It was early dawn and the eastern horizon was tinged pale pink when he felt Cobus prodding him with his bare foot.

"Come along," he said. "We have cows to milk, eggs to collect and chickens to feed."

Like Cobus, he had slept in his clothes, so it was a matter of a moment for Hennie to rub the sleep out of his eyes and follow. He stuck close to his cousin. Everything was very strange to him. Even the chickens scared him with their loud clucking and flapping of wings as he tried to remove the eggs from under them.

After delivering the eggs to the cooking shack, Hennie followed Cobus to the cowshed, where six black-and-white cows were placidly lining up, ready for their morning milking. Their mournful lowing raised the hackles on the back of Hennie's neck, and he panicked when Cobus told him to sit on the milking stool next to one of the cows.

Cobus washed his hands in the cold water of a bucket, dipped them into some oily looking yellow substance, kneeled down next to the stool, and demonstrated pulling the teats. The warm milk squirted into the pail, frothing as it started filling it up. Then he instructed Hennie to take over. Hennie's attempts to milk the cow made the herders laugh as they talked amongst themselves in Zulu. Hennie glared at the youngest herder, about seven or eight years old – his own age. The boy grinned back sheepishly.

After milking the other four cows, Cobus returned to finish Hennie's cow, which was looking around restlessly at Hennie's clumsy efforts. Hennie was mortified that he had not managed to coax a single stream of milk out of the cow's bulging udders. Cobus made it look so easy.

Hennie, sulking, made his way out of the milking shed but was stopped by Cobus, who dipped a tin mug into the brimming pail and held it out to him. The milk, still warm from the cows, was rich and creamy, and Hennie suddenly realised that he was starving.

Right on cue, a bell echoed over the field and Cobus grabbed Hennie's hand.

"Come on," he laughed. "I'll race you back to the house."

Without a second glance he sped off, with Hennie in pursuit.

Hennie had never seen so much food for breakfast before, but he had never been so hungry before. He smiled shyly at his cousin. He felt as if he and Cobus had become a team. Even the arrival of his stern uncle could not affect him when Cobus was at his side.

"Where is the milk?" asked Oom Jaco.

Cobus looked guiltily towards the milking shed where the milk had been left.

"I will go and fetch it, Pa," he said, and quickly jumped up to run to the milking shed.

He was not quick enough. His father's sjambok came down hard on his back as he tried to dodge out of the way. And then he was gone.

Oom Jaco called for his food, and a few minutes later Tant Sarie silently placed a loaded plate in front of him. He examined the offering for a moment before grunting and starting to eat.

As Oom Jaco finished his breakfast and wiped his mouth on his sleeve, he turned to glare at Hennie.

"You come with me," he said shortly.

They were the first words his uncle had spoken to him, and Hennie followed him quickly, taking three strides for each of his uncle's one. Stopping only to pick up a pick and a shovel, Oom Jaco made his way across the field, the small boy following at a trot, his bare feet padding silently on the dusty path. After about fifteen minutes at a cracking pace, Hennie saw that Cobus had joined them. Cobus gave him a grin as he came alongside his cousin. Oom Jaco glanced around briefly and saw his son. Without a word, he handed the pick to Cobus and carried on walking, with the boys keeping up as best they could.

They finally arrived at their destination. Oom Jaco was laying the foundations for a fence that would surround the farm, to which he had title. This involved digging deep holes for the droppers, setting them in place, then unwinding rolls of wicked-looking barbed wire and stringing the metal between the droppers. Two black farm workers were already digging, and Oom Jaco and Cobus joined them.

Hennie's job was to pack the soil into the holes around the droppers and tamp it down with another dropper. He had never done manual work before, and within a few hours his arms were aching and his hands were blistered and bleeding. He dared not utter a complaint and carried on as if his life depended on it.

The sun was at its peak when they stopped. Hennie was dripping with sweat that was running in rivulets through the dust caked on his bony chest. Oom Jaco and Cobus picked up their shirts and Cobus indicated that Hennie should follow him.

He set quite a pace, and the younger boy was ready to drop with exhaustion. But then they cleared a small rise, and Hennie saw the vlei in front of them, surrounded by bright green willow trees. Barely breaking his pace, Cobus dropped his shorts and was in the water before Hennie had even realised what was happening.

He needed no invitation. Within seconds he had joined his cousin, and soon lay almost completely submerged in the murky water. His hands were bleeding sluggishly and he moved them around to wash out the dried blood from between his fingers.

The sound of the bell peeling over the fields called them from their cool swim, and they shook the dust out of their shorts before pulling them on over their wet bodies.

Tant Sarie's usually sad face was transformed by a smile when she saw the boys arrive, their blonde hair tousled from the water. She placed a plate of steaming stew in front of each of them, accompanied by a pile of mealie pap.

The boys tucked in hungrily, watched at a safe distance by Cobus's sister, Nesta. According to tradition the males ate first, and only once they had finished did the females eat. Hennie was pleased to see that his uncle had already had his meal and gone for his midday rest.

When Tant Sarie saw Hennie's bleeding hands, she came out with a foul-smelling ointment which she rubbed onto the blisters, binding them with a flowery pink rag from what had long ago been her petticoat. Hennie resolved to remove the offending bandage as soon as she was out of sight.

It appeared that it was rest time for everyone on the farm, and Hennie followed Cobus to the stoep, unrolled his mattress and lay down. The chirping of the crickets and the lowing of the cows lulled him into sleep almost immediately.

A few hours later, after the heat of the day had abated, it was time to get up and feed the chickens and milk the cows again.

One day followed another in this manner, broken by Sundays, when they were solely permitted to tend to the animals. After their usual chores in the hen house and the dairy, and a hearty breakfast, the two boys washed under the cold water of the pump and changed their clothes. These clothes were then worn, day and night, until the following Sunday.

Sundays were Hennie's favourite. There was no field work, which he hated. However, it also meant that there was a three-hour study period with Tant Sarie, who taught them to read, write and do simple sums.

Hennie had spent two years at school before coming to the farm, and reading and writing were the only skills in which he was better than his older cousin. Nesta's lessons consisted of copying the letters that would form the basis of later reading skills.

Cobus battled with the words, but his mother's gentleness hid a core of steel, and there was no escape from the table until the work had been completed to her satisfaction.

This was followed in the evening by an hour-long Bible study period as Oom Jaco pretended to read passages out of the Bible. He had never learnt to read, and compensated for this by memorising whole passages by heart, making up the parts he had forgotten. Hennie pretended not to notice that the words were not the same as those that appeared on the pages of his Bible.

Sunday was also the only day that Hennie and Cobus were allowed into the house, and Hennie loved the cool darkness within.

The monotony of the farm was also broken by the three-day visit to Standerton for Nagmaal. This took place twice a year, and while the ostensible reason for this coming together of all the surrounding farmers and their families was to attend a church service and take communion, everyone knew that they were also there to enjoy themselves.

Farmer's wives in their Sunday best, donning snowy pinafores and caps, brought produce from their farms. Sheep were slaughtered and roasted slowly over fires which burned through the night, and distant neighbours reacquainted themselves with each other over roasted mutton and home-brewed liquor.

There was a regular programme of country dances and games, called volkspele. Older girls came dressed in traditional dresses with hand-crocheted collars and bonnets, while the younger girls had ribbons in their hair. Everywhere there was the sound of fiddles and accordions, and young people talking and laughing.

Farmers paraded skittish calves and fat cattle for sale, as well as strong bulls with fine pedigrees. There was also a brisk trade in marriageable daughters, and farmers with young sons were always on the lookout for potential mates for their heirs; robust young women who would work hard and provide grandsons to carry on the farming tradition.

Cobus and Hennie were growing up. Hennie was now twelve years old and Cobus, a stocky and handsome sixteen. Cobus spent his time with the teenage boys who showed off their riding skills to an admiring group of young girls under the watchful eyes of their mothers. Hennie followed them everywhere, jealous of all the time Cobus spent with these older boys and desperately trying to compete at their level.

Tant Sarie had dressed Nesta in a fine blue dress she had spent the winter months making, and Nesta's flaxen hair had been braided and threaded with blue ribbons. It was early days to be finding her a husband, she was only twelve years old, but in another two or three years she would be ready, and a little early grooming would not have been wasted.

Chapter 9

2010

Thuli was in her new house, surrounded by stepladders, paint and sandpaper. Cleaning the house had been a nightmare. The old man's wife had been dead for nineteen years, and to Thuli's fastidious eye it looked as if the house had not been cleaned since the day she died. Besides being full of an accumulation of a lifetime's worth of junk, it looked as if only surface dirt had been shifted during the past decade.

The outside of the house was already looking great. She had decided to get a professional painter in for that. The crisp white walls were offset by pale grey window frames which looked lovely with the dark slate roof. Once the garden was done, it would start to look every bit as good as the other houses in the road.

After clearing the house of all its junk, which took two skips, Thuli's first job inside was to remove all the appliances and built-in cupboards. Then she started cleaning. That took a full week and several broken fingernails. At last she had a clean canvas with which to start.

She had not seen Katie since the day after her father's stroke, but her friend had phoned with progress reports. Rick seemed to understand what they were saying, but he could not communicate. He seemed totally paralysed except for his face, which was badly twisted. Thuli was not sympathetic. Rick van Tonder had never liked her, and the feelings were completely reciprocated. He was a hard and morose man who seldom found anything that pleased him. She knew that Katie and Julie would miss him, but if he were her father, she would feel a sense of relief to escape his constant fault finding and disapproval.

Thuli had come across very little prejudice in her childhood and youth, with the notable exceptions of the men in Katie's family. She had the slight consolation of knowing that it was not she personally that brought this out in them. They were prejudiced against every person who was not white, male, Protestant, Afrikaans, South African, and born in the Transvaal. That meant blacks, women, Jews, Italians, Catholics, Indians, and anyone else who did not conform to this idea of a 'true South African'. The list of people they hated seemed endless, and Thuli often wondered how Katie had grown up so unbiased. Auntie Julie had obviously been her guiding influence.

Thuli had rarely been in their house when Rick van Tonder was not lecturing them about something. She got used to seeing Julie and Katie sitting sullenly silent while he held the floor. Although he had not made much of a success of himself in his hardware business, he was a petty tyrant in his own home.

This stroke must be driving Rick crazy, but it must definitely be an improvement for Katie and Julie, thought Thuli. She smiled as she imagined his frustration.

I hope he lives for another twenty years and never utters another word, she thought vindictively.

She picked up a piece of sandpaper and started sanding one of the many holes she had filled in the wall, bringing it to a smooth finish. She loved doing this sort of work. It was so therapeutic and calming.

A knock on the front door was quickly followed by a happy voice.

"Cooee, anybody home?"

Katie breezed in, a huge smile on her face, followed by her mother who was carrying a basket.

"We thought it was probably time for lunch. Do you feel like a picnic?"

"You wonderful, wonderful people!" answered Thuli, smiling. "There are garden chairs and a table outside, let's go and sit away from all this mess."

"Not until you have given me a tour," answered Katie. "I haven't been here since my grandmother died, but it feels like a totally different house already. It looks like a happy house."

"It will be," said Thuli determinedly.

They went through the house, first downstairs, and then up to the bedrooms. Katie happily recalled incidents from her childhood involving her loving and kind grandmother. She did not talk about her grandfather. He seemed to have been the root of many of the crises in her life and his treatment of her best friend had earned him her lifelong hatred.

She had always suspected that her grandmother's death that occurred when she was nine years old had been caused, directly or indirectly, by her grandfather.

"What are you planning?" Katie asked. "At the moment all I see is empty rooms. Which one is yours?"

"This one," answered Thuli, proudly showing a spacious north-facing room with a view of the garden, "and this one will be waiting for you to come and visit whenever you are in town."

They were both lovely airy rooms with en-suite bathrooms.

"And this is going to be my study," continued Thuli. "The bathrooms need to be totally gutted and redone, but I will start with this one." She indicated the bathroom next to her bedroom. "And the second one will be done when I have a little more money. Renovating an old house costs an extraordinary amount. Thank goodness I got the house for a good price."

"Actually, I was surprised to hear that my grandfather had gone into the retirement home," said Katie. "My father tried to get him to move into a smaller place after my grandmother died, but he always absolutely refused. He said he would die in this house."

"What made him change his mind?" asked Thuli.

"He didn't!" answered Katie. "He had a bad fall and broke his hip. Even after a month of physiotherapy it was obvious that he would be in a wheelchair for the rest of his life. That meant he wouldn't be able to get up and down the stairs. My father got the court to appoint him as my grandfather's guardian, and after that it was a simple matter to get him booked into the retirement home."

Thuli looked surprised. "Simple? I can't imagine it was simple to get him to actually move?"

"You are right about that. Apparently, it took them a good twenty minutes to get him out of the ambulance and into the retirement home. He thought they were taking him home after he was discharged and he became quite violent when he realised he was never coming back here."

Thuli shook her head, imagining the scene. Old as he must be, the memory of how formidable he had been frightened her like nothing else had ever done. She felt that by clearing out the house and making it her own she was taking the final step in exorcising that particular ghost.

They made their way down into the garden where Julie had laid out their picnic – homemade bread, fresh cold meats and salads, and homemade ginger beer. Julie was wandering around the garden, looking thoughtful.

"Thuli," she smiled, "what are you intending to do with this garden?"

"I am not really a gardener," answered Thuli. "I thought of getting a garden service in to rip everything out and start from scratch. It is totally overgrown and a real mess."

"Oh, but it was so beautiful, Thuli," said Julie sadly. "My mother-in-law was an amazing gardener. They moved in here after Hennie inherited the place, and although it was a much bigger house than they had before, the garden was non-existent. For some reason Hettie hated the house from the beginning, but she loved this garden, and soon it was the envy of everyone in town."

"I've been looking around, and most of the shrubs and trees she planted are still here, and salvageable. Before you decide to rip everything out, please talk to me. I'd love the opportunity to rescue this garden. It would be my tribute to a really lovely lady and a wonderful mother-in-law."

"That would be fantastic, Auntie Julie. I know nothing about gardening, so perhaps if you don't mind, you and I could work together so that I could learn how to take care of the garden myself once it's back to its old glory."

Julie beamed at her. She spent a good ten minutes pointing out rose bushes, honeysuckle, jasmine, oleanders and bougainvillea. She had always liked Thuli and thought that now perhaps, without Rick and his unaccountable prejudice, she would be able to spend some pleasant time in this garden and get to know Thuli better.

Julie and her mother-in-law had been a great comfort to each other over the years, after Rick's sister, Elmarie, had committed suicide. She had missed the old lady terribly since the fateful day she followed her daughter into the swift waters of the Vaal River, and, like Katie, Julie wondered whether there was not more to her death than her father-in-law maintained.

She looked at the two girls happily exchanging news. Tiny vivacious Katie with her long blonde hair and peachy complexion, and regal reserved Thuli with her warm coffee-coloured skin, high cheekbones and sleek dark hair caught back in a ponytail – total opposites to look at, but so complementary.

They sat down together, a happy little band of women, eating the picnic that Julie had prepared.

"What's going to happen now with your dad?" Thuli asked Katie. "Will he be coming out of hospital soon?"

"Well, actually," Katie answered for her mother, looking carefully at her sandwich, "the doctors say he is unlikely to improve. He will never be able to walk or talk again. It'll be impossible for him to take care of himself either physically or financially.

"So," she looked at Thuli with a guilty look, "we've booked him into the same retirement home as his father. I don't see why my mother should spend what is left of her life taking care of a man who treated her like a half-witted child all her life."

"Well, good for you!" Thuli reached across and took Julie's hand. Julie was looking a little embarrassed, yet excited at the same time. "You're doing the right thing, Auntie Julie. And Katie, I am proud of you, standing on your own feet and taking your future into your own hands."

"We have not told him yet. He's still in the hospital, but we thought that we'd take a leaf out of his own book and get the ambulance to take him straight to the retirement home from the hospital."

Katie looked nervous. "I dread being there when he discovers what we have done, but once we get over that hurdle it will be plain sailing."

Julie excused herself and went to walk around the garden again.

"What about the financial aspects?" Thuli was a bank manager, after all. She knew the value of money and the hardship that could be experienced in its absence.

"That's also good news. My father has a policy that pays out in the event of him becoming incapacitated. That, together with his pension, will give my mother a decent income for the rest of her life, as well as cover the retirement home costs. The house is paid off, so that's not an issue."

"And the business?" asked Thuli.

"At the moment, my father's assistant is keeping things going, but I've been approached by an estate agent who says he might have someone interested in taking over the name, the lease and the stock. It's in the early stages, but if he is willing to pay a fair price for it I think we'll sell."

"Well, it looks like you have covered all your bases," smiled Thuli. "Have you told your mother your news yet?"

They looked over at where Julie was wandering happily around the garden again.

"Yes," answered Katie. "It took a little bit of getting used to at first, but then she realised that she no longer has to worry about what my father thinks. So now she is very happy for me. We've already started setting dates and planning wedding outfits, and naturally you will be my maid of honour."

"I would indeed be honoured!" laughed Thuli. "What a happy ending."

"Not an ending, Thuli, a beginning," smiled Katie.

Chapter 10

1934

To Hennie, Cobus was a combination of big brother and guardian angel. He copied the way Cobus walked, talked ... even the way he whistled while he worked. Tant Sarie smiled when she saw the younger boy following his cousin like a puppy. She loved the boys. Her greatest joy was watching the two of them growing up together.

Hennie was thirteen years old and Cobus was seventeen when the first crack appeared in their friendship. Hennie had returned early from collecting the eggs. It was a beautiful clear day, with only a few small fluffy clouds in the sky. Hennie was itching to head down to the vlei for a swim. As usual, his first thought was to find Cobus, and he started searching in the yard around the house and then further afield. He finally found him in the orchard. He seemed to be struggling with someone he had pinned to the ground between the peach trees.

Innocently, Hennie called out.

"Hey, Cobus! Who have you got there? Is it a thief?"

Cobus turned to his cousin with a curse, but then rolled over, revealing Nesta beneath him, her skirts pulled up to show her naked legs and body. Her face was streaked with tears.

"What are you doing?"

"Go away! This has nothing to do with you," snarled Cobus, pulling on his shorts and heading towards the vlei.

Nesta quickly pulled down her skirts, drying her eyes on her sleeves. She got to her feet and turned her back on Hennie.

"Please don't say anything, Hennie. Pa will kill me if he finds out."

"Finds out what?" asked Hennie, confused.

Nesta turned to look at him disbelievingly, suspecting that he was mocking her. She could not believe that he really did not know what had been happening.

"Nothing! Just say nothing about anything."

Forgetting her instantly, Hennie turned and ran towards the vlei, hoping to see Cobus and find out what he had done to offend him. But Cobus had disappeared. This was the first time that his hero had been angry with him. Hennie's only thought was to beg Cobus's forgiveness for upsetting him, and to have his best friend back.

He waited until the evening meal was done, prayers were said, and Oom Jaco and Tant Sarie could be heard snoring gently inside. It was a typically magnificent Transvaal night. The dark-blue velvet sky was pierced with stars that cast a silvery glow over the yard, making it appear like something out of a fairy tale. Hennie should have been enjoying it. Instead, he was miserable in his isolation from the person he loved most in the world.

The two boys lay on their mattresses on the stoep, Cobus being stubbornly silent. Hennie simply could not bear it. Finally, he plucked up the courage to speak.

"Cobus, are you awake?" he asked.

When no reply came after a minute, he said again, "Cobus?"

"What do you want?" snarled Cobus.

"I want to say I'm sorry. I didn't know you were busy."

"What do you mean busy?" whispered Cobus angrily.

"I don't know ... playing with Nesta?" answered Hennie uncertainly.

"Playing?" Cobus laughed shortly. "You think we were playing?"

"Ye-es?" answered Hennie hesitantly.

"Well, I suppose you could call it playing."

Hennie mused over this answer.

"Why was Nesta crying?"

"Girls cry. That's what girls do," Cobus snapped. "Now go to sleep. We'll be digging the western boundary tomorrow and you'll need to be fresh."

Happy that they appeared to be friends again, Hennie drifted off to sleep, but his dreams were haunted by the image of the shame on Nesta's tear-streaked face.

In a few days the friendship between the boys resumed its normal course, and Hennie soon forgot the incident in the orchard. His only disappointment was that he was seeing less of his cousin. Cobus seemed restless like the cows on a stormy night. He had taken to disappearing on his own after they had settled for the night, and he refused to take Hennie with him.

After the next Nagmaal, and shortly before his eighteenth birthday, Cobus became even more elusive. He seemed to have changed; to have become a man rather than a boy.

Hennie missed all the time they usually spent together, and longed for a return to the easy friendship that they had shared. It was inevitable that things would come to a head.

It was early evening and Hennie was returning from feeding the chickens, a basket of eggs in hand, when he heard muffled noises. Following the noise, he saw a familiar sight that stopped him in his tracks.

Cobus had cornered Nesta, this time in the milking shed, and was grunting as he rammed his body into hers. Nesta was sobbing, trying to fight him off.

35

Cobus hit her hard across the face, slamming her head against the feed trough and momentarily stunning her. Hennie watched, a mixture of fascination and horror rooting him to the spot.

Suddenly aware that he had gained an audience, Cobus turned around to see Hennie, his eyes wide and his face shocked. Frightened of offending Cobus, Hennie turned to leave, but Cobus called him back.

Keeping his forearm against his sister's throat, he grinned at Hennie. "Come on, boetie, you're old enough now. Do you want a turn?"

"To do what?" asked Hennie.

Cobus laughed and beckoned Hennie over.

"Don't be so dense. You've seen the bull with the cows and the cock with the hens. What do you think they're doing? Ja! This is exactly the same. Now, are you ready?"

He rolled off his sister without releasing her neck. He kept the pressure on her throat and with her arms trapped above her head, the threat clear.

"But ... Nesta," said Hennie uncertainly, looking at his cousin's tear-soaked face. "I don't think she wants me to."

"Forget what Nesta thinks. She's just a girl. This is what girls are for. God put them on earth for men to use ... to work, to cook and to fuck. Are you going to question God?"

Fearful of upsetting a terrible God and desperate not to offend his hero again, Hennie obediently dropped his ragged shorts and straddled Nesta's writhing body as Cobus had done, avoiding the kicks that she aimed at him.

"What am I supposed to do?" he mumbled, embarrassed, his limp penis slapping uselessly against Nesta's bare legs.

"Hennie, don't listen to him! Please, don't do it," pleaded Nesta through her tears.

"Nothing happening?" laughed Cobus sympathetically. "Don't worry, boetie. This is your first try. It will be better next time. You just need to practise on your own a bit. Come, I will show you how."

The two boys walked off amicably, talking about the intricacies of sex and masturbation, while Nesta dried her tears and straightened her dress. Again she considered the possibility of telling her mother, but rejected the idea as foolhardy. Girls were supposed to be virgins when they got married. She would have no chance of finding a husband and leaving this cursed farm if anyone found out that she was being raped by her brother on a regular basis. And now it seemed like another tormenter was going to join him.

Hennie's second attempt at rape some three weeks later was only slightly more successful, but to Hennie it was a major achievement. Cobus trapped her in the shed and held her down while Hennie made his play. Nesta fought wildly, and this was all the stimulation Hennie needed. Although he failed to penetrate his cousin, he did achieve an orgasm, and afterwards stood over her panting with exertion. Grinning triumphantly, Hennie left her furious and vengeful lying on the hay in the milking shed. Now he was a man, like Cobus. Cobus slapped him on the back, welcoming him to an elite club.

With Hennie now obsessed with catching Nesta unawares, Cobus appeared to lose all interest in her. Nesta was relieved at his lack of interest and concentrated her efforts on avoiding any chance of encountering Hennie. Unfortunately, this would not always be possible, as her duties took her to all parts of the homestead.

In between avoiding her cousin, Nesta racked her brain to find a way to permanently discourage Hennie. A few days later, she had an inspiration. Womanlike, she understood that Hennie was young and insecure, trying desperately to be like his big swaggering cousin. So she decided to play on these insecurities.

She was on her way to the milking shed with a clean pail for the evening's milking when she spotted Hennie watching from behind the bushes. Taking a deep breath and praying that her theory was right, she marched boldly up to him, the smile of contempt on her face hiding her fear.

"Come on, little boy, do you want to try again, or can you only be a man when Cobus is there to help you? Maybe you will get it right this time." She pulled up her skirts. "Come along, boetie. Try to prove yourself a man. Hah! Just look at you, pathetic! You are nothing but a little boy with a little pipi." She waggled her little finger at him mockingly.

"Cobus and I laugh at you when we're together. You and your little boy's pipi! He makes an impression on a girl. But you, you are nothing. A child, a baby."

She laughed derisively and turned her back on him.

Hennie stood rooted to the spot, blood rushing to his face and tears to his eyes. This was not how it was supposed to be. Girls were supposed to be submissive and cry, not mock and torment. His urge to grab his young cousin disappeared and was replaced by an even stronger urge to run. He fled, the sound of her mocking laughter following him all the way to the house.

Hennie still watched Nesta from behind the bushes, and she was well aware that he was there, but he no longer tried to corner her. Her mocking smile and waggling little finger were enough to put him off forever, and his embarrassment ensured that he never mentioned the incident to Cobus.

Chapter 11

2010

It took Thuli almost six months and a lot more money than she had budgeted to get the house ready for occupation. At the same time, she worked closely with Julie to organise Katie's wedding.

Two months after announcing her engagement, Katie was called away unexpectedly on a very lucrative contract – a series of photo shoots in eight different exotic locations. The locations were remote and inaccessible, and the work was both demanding and glamorous. As this had kept her pretty much out of contact for the four months immediately prior to the wedding, Julie and Thuli had ended up doing most of the organising.

Katie had no doubt that they would be able to manage things in her absence and gave them carte blanche with the arrangements. Her one exception was the wedding dress. One of the designers she worked with had offered to make her dress, and even Thuli was being kept in the dark. Katie's only stipulation was that the theme colour of the wedding should be shades of antique gold.

Katie arrived back in Standerton a few short days before the wedding to put the final touch to the arrangements but could find no fault with what they had planned.

Thuli looked at her watch and rushed upstairs to get ready. She had organised a spa day for Katie's hen party and was picking her up in a few minutes. It was also an excuse to get her away from Patrick, who had been monopolising her since his arrival two weeks before.

Patrick was just as Thuli remembered him – big, quiet and shy – and definitely not her idea of a football star. She thought her friend would be very happy with her childhood sweetheart, but she was a little bit jealous too. Although Thuli did have the odd short romance when she was growing up, she never found anyone who matched the image she held in her heart. She hoped that one day she would be the one walking down the aisle, with Katie as her maid of honour.

Uncharacteristically, Katie was ready when Thuli pulled up at her front door. Patrick came to the door with her, very reluctant to allow her to be driven away.

"You will see her tomorrow as she walks down the aisle!" Thuli shouted as she put her foot on the accelerator, making their escape.

Thuli was determined to make this last twenty-four hours special for Katie. She was pleased to see Julie and two of Katie's friends waiting for them when they arrived at the spa. A few minutes later, the wives of three of Patrick's footballer friends arrived. Thuli had been dreading meeting them, expecting arrogant little princesses, too spoilt to join in the fun. The opposite was true. The three young women were excited to see Katie again after such a long absence, and soon they were all gossiping happily together. The scene was set for a perfect hen party.

"Nails first, I think," said Thuli imperiously, clapping her hands together like an impresario, "then the steam room, a quick swim, then either a full body massage, aromatherapy or reflexology, followed by a fabulous and healthy lunch. Then there is time for a short snooze next to the pool, followed by the hairdressers and a pedicure. How does that sound?"

"Bliss!" Katie's laughter was echoed by that of the others. "I could definitely get used to this sort of pampering."

The women each went off with a personal beautician. By the end of the day they had all become friends, and Katie was happy and relaxed. Worth every penny, thought Thuli contentedly.

Katie looked radiant as she came down the aisle the following day, holding her mother's arm. They had considered bringing Rick to the wedding but the doctor had said that he was too ill to attend the service, even in a wheelchair, and Julie was happy to give away the bride.

Katie's dress was simple and elegant, the soft ivory satin trimmed with old gold lace hugging her figure and setting off her blonde hair to perfection. Instead of a veil she wore a crown of tiny yellow rosebuds, delicate little first-love proteas, and gypsophila. Julie and Thuli were dressed in complementary shades; Julie in an elegant linen suit in soft amber; Thuli in a slim sheath dress of primrose yellow, mirroring the slim lines of Katie's wedding gown.

"One day," thought Thuli as she followed her friend down the aisle, "that will be me. All I need to do now is to find the right man."

She smiled at her grandmother as she passed her. She could see that her grandmother was thinking exactly the same thing.

Patrick had also brought a touch of glamour with him, as his family party was joined by the three football stars and their wives. From the smiles they gave Katie as she passed by, Thuli was in no doubt that Katie would be welcomed into their midst. She only hoped that Katie would not give up her promising career for the life of a WAG.

After the reception, Katie and Patrick left for a week in Madagascar, returning for a few hours to see Julie and Thuli.

And then they were gone.

Chapter 12

Several days later, Thuli stood on her patio sipping strong black coffee and looking at her garden, still wild and untamed. Although the house was now pretty much as she wanted it, the garden had been put on the backburner while the wedding preparations were in progress.

Knowing that Julie would be finding life as dull as she was, now that the wedding was over, Thuli decided to follow up on Julie's offer of working on the garden. She picked up her phone and soon had arranged for Julie to come over on Friday after she was home from work. They would then set up a plan of action for the weekend.

"I'm so glad you phoned me, Thuli," said Julie gratefully, a few days later. "I've been dreading being on my own in the house, now that Katie and Patrick are back in London."

"This suits us both, I think," laughed Thuli. "I've also been feeling a bit flat since they left."

They were both covered in scratches from the rose bushes they had been pruning. Black bags full of grass cuttings and branches of various bushes were leaning against the garden wall, awaiting removal to the dump.

The garden was showing signs of what it had once been, and both Thuli and Julie were feeling a justifiable sense of achievement.

Gogo came into the garden with a glass of water for each of them.

"Time for a break," she said. "First a drink to refresh you, then you can go and wash your hands for lunch."

Gogo was an excellent cook, and Thuli and Julie needed no second invitation.

"You have been working non-stop on this house, Thuli, and now the garden. When are you going to stop this hard work and just relax in your new home? You work so hard during the week and then you come home and work even harder. It's time to slow down."

Gogo was a straight talker, but Thuli was the one person who had always been able to charm her.

"I'll have enough time to relax when I'm in my grave," she answered mischievously.

"Aish!" laughed Gogo, acknowledging the hit. That was Gogo's stock answer when people advised her to slow down, or when Thuli complained about the pace her grandmother set.

"You are too much like your grandmother, perhaps!" Gogo laughed.

"I really am enjoying my new home, Gogo. I find that working on the house and the garden is the best way to relax. But as much as we have already done, there is still so much I want to do."

"Oh, but it's already perfect," exclaimed Julie. "I can't believe it is the same tired-looking place you bought. It has such a happy feel to it now. When my father-in-law was living here, I used to dread our visits. He always intimidated me, but more so after my mother-in-law had died. He seemed more reserved and angry, somehow. I suppose he missed her, though I never thought he was very nice to her when she was alive. Rickie said he was different before Elmarie died. After she committed suicide, he changed completely."

"Some men don't know how to cope with their feelings," suggested Gogo kindly.

"Oh, he knew how to show his feelings," said Thuli emphatically. "I remember one day so vividly, when Katie and I were only about eight years old. Auntie Julie had brought us with her when she came to visit Katie's granny. Katie and I were playing hide and seek. I went off and hid in the garage, and Katie was taking ages to find me. Then I heard someone come in, and I stood up to see if it was Katie. But it was the grandfather.

"He stood absolutely still and stared at me with his mouth open, like I was some kind of ghost. He had a look of horror on his face and just stared. Eventually, I asked him if he had seen Katie. Suddenly, he seemed to snap. He grabbed me by my arm, really hurting me, and dragged me out. He was shouting like a mad thing all the way. He told me to stay away from him!"

"I remember it as if it was yesterday," said Julie. "He was totally hysterical. I had never really experienced racism until that day, but that is the only explanation for his reaction to finding you there. I couldn't understand it as you had been there so often previously."

"You never told me that!" exclaimed Gogo.

"I suppose I was too ashamed. I felt as if I had done something wrong. That was the last time I ever went into that house. I mean, this house, of course ... until the day I walked in as the owner! I suppose it was silly of me, but I was so traumatised about being thrown out of the house that, when I wanted to buy a house, this was the very house I wanted. It was as if I wanted to prove I was good enough to live here."

Gogo looked around the house, shaking her head in amazement at the transformation that had taken place.

"I still wonder sometimes if you did the right thing to buy this house. You have changed it completely and made it your own, but ..." She trailed off uncertainly, not even knowing herself what she meant.

41

"Don't say anything negative about my lovely new house!" laughed Thuli. "I'm really very happy here, and although I did buy it partly to get my revenge on Katie's grandfather, that is totally irrelevant now. It's my house and I love it."

"It's certainly unrecognisable as the old place, both inside and out," said Julie. "I can't imagine how you think you could still improve it."

"Actually, I've already decided on my next project," said Thuli mysteriously. "You know I have been saying I need a laundry? Well, I went to the council offices yesterday and picked up a copy of the plans of the house."

She brought out a roll of plans and laid them out, moving crockery and cutlery out of the way as she spread the plans onto the large glass table. The women crowded around to have a look.

"Looking at the old house plans, you can see that there used to be a laundry here, between the garage and the house.

"Well, somehow, it's no longer there. The plans were drawn up a long time ago, and I suppose it might have been built differently, or the laundry was incorporated into the garage or kitchen. But the plans and the building just don't seem to match.

"I'm getting a builder to see whether he can either find where the old laundry was, or build me a new one. These days, nobody drives those huge old American cars and I only have one car after all. So the garage is definitely big enough to block a section off to make a laundry, though it would be great to find the site of the original laundry. It would probably have all the original plumbing installed and could save me a fortune."

They pored over the plans, trying to work out the size of the various rooms. Thuli even fetched her grandmother's measuring tape from her sewing basket to try to work out the dimensions, but since it was only one metre long, they were not very successful. It was all very intriguing and frustrating.

As Thuli needed to be at work during the week, Julie offered to stay at the house with the builder.

Two days later, she was seated comfortably on the patio, reading a book to the accompaniment of hammering from the garage where the builder was smashing a large hole through the wall. After less than an hour, the noise stopped. Becoming aware of the silence, Julie looked up to see the builder standing at the patio door, holding his hammer limply at his side, looking dazed.

"Mrs van Tonder," he said quietly, "I think we need to call the police."

"What? Why?" Julie was totally taken aback.

"I have found some bones," he answered hoarsely.

"What kind of bones? Why would we call the police for some bones?"

"No, no! You don't understand," he said desperately, trying very hard to stay calm. "These are human bones."

"Nonsense, there are no graves here!" she laughed merrily. "This was my father-in-law's house, and he would have told us."

"I can assure you, Mrs van Tonder, I have been in the army and have seen some terrible things in my time, and I know what human remains look like. Can we please call the police? I don't want the responsibility of this any longer. I want the police here, now."

It was the fear and horror on his face that finally galvanised Julie into action. She picked up the phone and dialled the emergency number, panic and dread making her fingers clumsy.

Having called the police emergency number, she also placed a call to Thuli's office. Thuli was in a meeting with a client, and under normal circumstances Julie would have left a message. However, these were definitely not normal circumstances. She asked the secretary to call Thuli out of the meeting. She said that Thuli should return home immediately; that it was an emergency. Then she sat down, trying to calm her overactive imagination and work out what the implications of this discovery might be.

Thuli arrived about fifteen minutes later, expecting to see water shooting up from a pipe, or a collapsed wall. As she pulled into her driveway, a good looking man was climbing out of a car in front of her house. She shot him an admiring backward glance before running up the path. Julie met her at the door, horror on her face. She clutched Thuli's hands.

"What is it?" asked Thuli, trying to understand Julie's frozen expression.

"Bones!" uttered Julie faintly. "He found bones."

Thuli looked around and saw the builder, standing just inside the patio door, holding his hat in both hands and looking out of place in her feminine sitting room.

She was about to question him when a knock at the open door behind her revealed the man from the car outside.

"Mrs van Tonder?" he asked politely.

"That is me," answered Julie, "but this is not my house, it's Thuli's house, Thuli Nyembe." She indicated Thuli, who turned to shake his offered hand.

"Detective Malepo," he said, flipping open his badge momentarily to show his credentials.

"What's this all about?" he asked, but Thuli shrugged and shook her head, looking around at the builder for an explanation.

"I think I should show you first, Detective," he said. "I don't want to upset the womenfolk."

Thuli stepped forward, bristling. Like many bright and ambitious young women, she resented the implication that she was a member of the 'weaker' gender.

"Detective, if there is something wrong with my house, mere woman or not, I would like to know about it. I'm coming with you."

Malepo turned to face her.

"No. I am sorry miss," he said respectfully. "Once I have established exactly what we have here, we can talk. But until that time, I must ask you and Mrs van Tonder to wait in the sitting room, please."

He turned and followed the builder through to the garage, leaving Thuli fuming.

"What a flaming cheek," she snapped angrily, "telling me what to do in my own home!"

"Thuli, darling," said Julie nervously, clutching Thuli's arm. "I really think we should listen to the nice detective."

"Well, I don't!" said Thuli angrily, and was about to follow them to the garage.

"Please don't leave me here alone!" cried Julie, desperately.

Thuli turned to see that Julie was seriously distressed.

"Oh, Auntie Julie! I'm so sorry. Of course I'll stay." She held Julie's hands, and felt them shaking.

"Now what is this about bones?"

"The builder said he had found human bones."

"Here? In my house?"

"I really don't know. He just came in looking frightened and asked me to call the police because he had found human bones."

"It's probably a cat that got stuck in a pipe or something, twenty years ago. Honestly Auntie Julie, I'm sure it's nothing to worry about."

Thuli put her arm around Julie's shoulders and led her to the couch. "I'm going to make you a strong cup of tea, and when the detective returns you will see that I'm right."

She went through to the kitchen and switched on the kettle. As it boiled, she craned her neck to look through the window towards the garage but could not see any sign of either the builder or the detective.

Thuli carried the tea tray through to the sitting room where Julie was sitting in exactly the same position staring out into the garden. She coaxed Julie to drink the sweet tea to counter her shock.

After what seemed like an hour, Detective Malepo returned to the room, taking Thuli's elbow and steering her into the kitchen.

"Miss Nyembe," he said quietly, "is there somewhere you can stay for a few weeks?"

"Weeks? Detective, what is this all about? You can't just ask me to move out of my home without telling me what's going on."

"Well, I can tell you that what the builder said was correct. There are human bones, and it appears that we have a crime scene."

Thuli stared at him, not believing her ears. This was her darling little house that she had spent the past six months renovating and restoring, and here was this Denzel Washington lookalike saying that she had been living with a corpse!

"I have called my headquarters and we'll soon have a team of investigators arriving to secure the site and collect any evidence."

"This is just not possible," Thuli said, shaking her head.

"Tell me, Miss, how long have you lived here?"

"Just over six months," she answered dully. She could hear the blood roaring through her ears, and her voice sounded faint and distant to her. "I bought the house on auction. I have just spent my life's savings and the past six months turning it into my dream home."

She gave him a frozen smile, and felt her knees give under her as she sank unconscious to the ground.

Chapter 13

1938

Nagmaal would never be the same for Hennie. The Nagmaal of 1938 heralded huge changes in their lives. Nesta, at the age of fifteen, was considered old enough to marry. She was a pretty girl, strong and sturdy, with thick blonde plaits which her mother wound around her head in a coronet. Finding her a husband was a simple matter. Tant Sarie was pleased to see that Nesta was entering into the spirit of the project with enthusiasm and had managed to attract the attention of one of the most eligible bachelors in the area.

The fathers of the two young people met to draw up the contract. Cattle passed hands, and within four days Nesta left the Nagmaal, married to the darkly handsome Tertius Serfontein, twenty years old and the sole heir to an adjacent farm. Hennie's heart was torn to see her go. It was not just those few moments he had stolen in the milking shed that he would miss. In his own way, he felt a real affection for his cousin.

As the young couple mounted their cart and started off on their new life together, Hennie waved goodbye. Nesta did not return the wave, but turned her head towards her young husband and her new life. It could only be better than the old.

Cobus was twenty, old enough to find himself a wife. But his father had as yet made no provision for his son's future. It was tradition among the local farmers for a house to be built on the farm when a son reached marriageable age. Without it, a man could not bring home a bride.

Cobus was furious. Not only was his younger sister getting married to a wealthy farmer, but all his friends were also finding wives. He watched all the prettiest girls being snapped up one by one, and eventually decided to broach the matter with his father.

"Patience, son," answered Oom Jaco. "I only married your mother when I was twenty-two years old. You have plenty of time. If you like, we can start building your house next winter, after we have finished clearing the eastern mealie fields."

Cobus was not happy with this reply but he knew that it was pointless to argue. His father controlled the purse strings and rarely parted with a penny. All the family funds were kept locked in a strongbox under his father's bed, together with the family Bible and other important papers.

He could argue all he wanted but Cobus knew it was an argument he would not win. The strongbox was untouchable and out of his reach. The key hung on a chain around Oom Jaco's neck, next to his heart.

Hennie, on the other hand, was delighted that Cobus's marriage seemed to be indefinitely postponed. The thought of his cousin bringing home a wife, and no longer wishing for the company of a cousin four years his junior, gave him nightmares.

But Cobus was restless and resentful. He spent the remainder of the Nagmaal week hanging around the less salubrious areas of the town, and often did not return all night. Oom Jaco was occupied with organising his daughter's wedding and did not have much time to worry about an angry and rebellious son.

After they returned to the farm, Cobus started disappearing at night after his parents' candle had been extinguished. He only reappeared hours later, sometimes with the dawn. He was moody, and often cut short his cousin's happy banter with a curse. Hennie suggested accompanying him on his outings, but was firmly rebuffed. He missed their easy camaraderie. He felt hurt, and lonelier than he had ever felt before.

It was a hot summer's night, about six weeks after Nagmaal. Hennie woke to find Cobus standing at his side. He seemed to be in high spirits and smelled strange to Hennie, like communion wine.

"Wake up, boetie. Do you want to have some fun?" he whispered hoarsely.

"Sure!" answered Hennie, jumping up eagerly and following as Cobus made his way through the yard towards the nearby workers' village. He was thrilled that Cobus had sought out his company and trotted along happily in his cousin's wake. As they left the yard, Cobus stopped and picked up a bottle from behind the water barrel. He took a long swig and passed the bottle to Hennie.

"Drink!" he ordered. Hennie obediently drank, choking on the raw alcohol in the bottle.

"What is it?" he spluttered when he had caught his breath.

"Witblits – white lightning," laughed Cobus unsteadily, tipping the bottle into his cousin's mouth for a second slug of the harsh liquid.

"Where did you get it?" asked Hennie, trying desperately not to choke.

"There is a man in Bethel who makes it. I bought some at the last Nagmaal. Don't tell my father."

"Of course not!" said Hennie indignantly, shocked that Cobus could even imagine that he would betray him.

"Where are we going?" he asked breathlessly, taking another gulp from the bottle.

"To have some fun," answered Cobus. "Come with me, and be quiet."

Walking very carefully, they approached the sleeping village. Cobus checked that there was no one on guard, and motioned Hennie to stay back. Then he carefully crossed the open ground between the bushes and the village. He leaned through the doorway of the closest hut and peered inside. Shaking his head and with exaggerated caution, he walked to the second hut, his finger to his lips. This time he was in luck – it was the women's hut. Cobus crept in and grabbed the closest girl, clapping his hand over her mouth to stifle her screams and carried her out into the warm night air.

Whooping with excitement, he carried the struggling child towards the vlei, with Hennie bringing up the rear. She was very small, probably only about eight years old, but that did not worry Cobus. He soon had her pinned under him, wildly forcing himself into her small body and hitting her viciously as she struggled to free herself. After a few minutes he rolled off her, laughing hysterically.

"Come on, boetie, she's all yours," he shouted, and watched as Hennie took his turn raping the now unresponsive child.

Satisfied, they left the child lying on the ground. Still clutching the bottle, and with their arms around each other for support, they started back to the house. Suddenly, they found their way barred by a dark silent figure. It was one of the farm workers who had heard the noise and come out to investigate.

Cobus did not waste time with words. With a single swing, he knocked the young man to the ground with the now-empty bottle. He grabbed Hennie's arm and they raced back to the house whooping with laughter.

Excitement bubbled up in Hennie as they ran. This was living life on the edge. He had never felt more alive or more powerful.

Dawn brought sobriety and reason. It also brought the chief from the village. The old man was clothed in full ceremonial dress. His springbok-skin loincloth hung to his knees. He had a tall black hat on his head, and a cape of springbok skin hung from his back. He carried his shield and spear. The chief was flanked by two younger men, one of whom had a bleeding gash on the side of his head.

Oom Jaco emerged from inside the house, perplexed at the formality of this visit. He greeted the stern old man and indicated some stools under the acacia tree where they could talk, man to man.

Cobus beckoned to Hennie and they quickly retreated together to behind the milking shed. From there they had a vantage point and could follow the proceedings, which continued for several hours. It was obvious that serious matters were being discussed. Oom Jaco looked grim as he opened the gate to the cow pasture and selected one of the milking cows, which he led out and handed over to the old man.

One of the younger men took possession of the cow and led it back towards the village as Oom Jaco and the chief concluded their discussions. As the chief and his party left, Oom Jaco looked around him for the instigators of the mischief.

"Let's get out of here," hissed Cobus, and they ran as far as they could from the farmhouse.

It was dark and both boys were starving when they finally returned to the house. As they came round the corner and mounted the stairs to the stoep, they saw Oom Jaco sitting in the shadows, rocking on his chair and smoking his pipe. They reluctantly approached, stopping in front of him.

Oom Jaco looked at the two boys as if he was seeing them for the first time.

"Do you know that the girl died?" he asked quietly.

"No, Pa," answered Cobus in a strangled voice. "We didn't mean to kill her, honestly. We were just having a bit of fun."

"Well, your bit of fun has cost me one of my best cows and has upset the chief of the village. That was his granddaughter you killed."

"Sorry, Pa. Sorry, Oom," they said simultaneously.

"You!" said Oom Jaco, turning and pointing a bony finger at Hennie, frightening him half to death. "You are young and inexperienced. I have no doubt you were led on by Cobus. I hope you have learnt your lesson."

"Yes, Oom," answered Hennie soberly, his voice breaking over the words.

Oom Jaco turned to Cobus with a look that boded ill for his son.

"You, I will deal with in the morning."

Without another word, he turned and left them on the stoep.

Hennie was sure he would be unable to sleep, but the disturbed night and the long day on the run had tired him out, and he slept soundly.

Cobus was not so lucky. His father was stern and autocratic, and was infuriated by anything that cost him money. Cobus was sure that the punishment would be harsh. He eventually fell asleep, intending to escape before his father arose in the morning. Unfortunately for him, he was still fast asleep when he felt his father's boot nudging him.

"Get up!" his father commanded contemptuously.

Cobus clambered awkwardly to his feet, cursing the fact that he had overslept. His heart sank when he saw that his father was carrying his sjambok. The whip was over a metre long and made of supple cow hide. Cobus tried to run, but his father was clutching his shoulder in a vice-like grip, his fingernails digging into his bare flesh.

He pulled Cobus towards the pump and tied the young man's hands together with a leather strap, which he then fastened to the pump. Raising the sjambok, he brought it down twenty times on his son's back until the blood trickled down into the waistband of his shorts. Hennie cowered on his mattress, watching in horror as his cousin was beaten until he collapsed onto the ground.

"The next time you want a bit of fun, don't look for it on my farm."

Cobus lay where he had fallen, his back a network of bleeding lines.

"You will go and tend to the animals." Oom Jaco growled as he returned to the farmhouse. Hennie ran to do his bidding. He was afraid that his uncle would remember that he, too, had been involved in the incident and would mete out the same punishment to him.

Hennie returned to the house to eat his lunch, and then his supper, his duties around the farm keeping him busier than usual as he was also doing tasks usually undertaken by Cobus. It was late when he finished for the day. Tant Sarie had kept some food for him which he ate with one eye on his cousin and the other on his uncle, who sat in his usual spot on the stoep.

Cobus had managed to crawl to his mattress on the stoep. He lay on his stomach, the flies buzzing around the bloody weals on his back. As the sun set, Oom Jaco and Tant Sarie prepared themselves for bed. After Hennie had watched them settle down for the night, he brought a cloth and some water from the pump and attempted to wash the wounds on his cousin's back.

Cobus angrily pushed him away.

"Leave it!" he snarled.

"But ..."

"Just leave me alone. I don't need any of your help."

Rebuffed, Hennie stood around awkwardly for a few minutes, not knowing what to do. But Cobus ignored him, turning his face to the wall. Hennie finally settled himself down and, despite the events of the previous few days, was soon asleep.

He awoke a few hours later to darkness, the smell of smoke and the sound of screaming coming from the workers' village. Sitting up, his first thought was to wake Cobus. But Cobus's mattress was empty. Sounds from inside the house indicated that his uncle had also woken. A moment later, Oom Jaco emerged, carrying a hurricane lantern. He looked around for the boys, but seeing only Hennie, beckoned for him to follow.

They ran towards the village. The sky was illuminated, and the sound of crackling flames and of women wailing could be heard as they got closer. The village was in mourning. Women and children stood around the edge of the gathering. The women were ululating; a sound that made Hennie's hair rise all over his body.

The men stood shoulder to shoulder around a figure lying in the middle of the clearing. At the arrival of Oom Jaco and Hennie, they turned silently but accusingly to face them. Two of the huts had been set alight and the roof trusses were still burning, the glowing reeds dropping to the ground. Only the charred mud walls remained standing.

According to custom, Oom Jaco stood at the edge of the village and asked to see the chief. Silently, the men parted ranks, giving Oom Jaco a clear view of the figure on the ground. It was the lifeless body of the old man, his spear embedded deep in his chest.

Oom Jaco took a few steps back, his horror twofold. He had no doubt as to who was responsible, but asked anyway.

"Who did this?" he croaked, the Zulu language unfamiliar on his tongue.

"It was the young master," replied one of the men. "He came in the night like an assassin and dragged my father, the chief, from his hut. Then he killed him with his own spear. I was too late to stop him, but I saw it with my own eyes."

"Cobus!" whispered Oom Jaco chokingly to himself. "Oh, my son, what have you done?"

"He must pay the price!" demanded the chief's son. "A life for a life!"

Oom Jaco stood for a few minutes in silence, pondering the implications of the situation.

"I will be back at first light," he promised as he turned towards the house, Hennie following silently behind.

They returned to find Tant Sarie brewing coffee in the cooking shack. Her usually tight bun was loose, and her hair hung over one shoulder in a long thick plait, the black already streaked with grey. Her pinafore was tied over her nightdress. She looked like a young woman, vulnerable and frightened, in the flickering light of the fire.

"Has Cobus been here?" demanded Oom Jaco as he entered the shack.

"He has come, and he has gone," she replied quietly, her pale face streaked with unfamiliar tears. "He said that he was leaving and that he was taking his inheritance with him."

Oom Jaco paused in shock for only a second, then turned and ran to the house. A roar of fury sounded from within. He emerged with his strongbox, the lock shattered and the lid twisted at an unlikely angle.

The Bible and the papers lay undisturbed. The money was all gone, every last penny; a lifetime of hard work and thrift, gone in an instant.

Checking further, Oom Jaco found that the money was not all that Cobus had taken. His rifle and his favourite horse were also missing, with its fine saddle and brasses.

Tant Sarie cried silently, and Oom Jaco put his hand on her shoulder.

"Come wife, we need to talk."

Hennie sat on the small stool, listening to the muted sounds of voices from within. Oom Jaco's deep voice was angry and purposeful, while Tant Sarie's was tearful and pleading. As the eastern sky lightened, Oom Jaco emerged, looking grim. He set off on the path to the village. Hennie started to follow, but was ordered back.

"You tend to your duties, boy!" snapped his uncle. Hennie turned with a heavy heart to perform his tasks. The chickens fed, he went to the milking shed. The cows were not waiting, and he could hear them lowing in the field near the vlei. The farmhands were not working today.

Hennie picked a branch from the willow tree to use as a whip, and led the remaining cows through to the milking shed. Having to herd, feed and milk the cows was a big job for one boy, and by the time he had returned the cows to the field and swept out the milking shed, it was almost midday.

He carried the milk pail to the farmhouse, and ate a late breakfast. His uncle had still not returned from the village, and Tant Sarie looked worried. Eventually, she could stand it no longer.

"Hennie, go to the village and see what is keeping Oom Jaco," she asked.

Hennie was on his way in a heartbeat. Although it was no great distance to the village, today it seemed very far away. As he approached, he saw his uncle walking towards him, shoulders bowed under the weight of his sorrow.

Reaching Hennie, he stopped. Then he put his hand on Hennie's shoulder.

"I am glad you are here, Hendrik. I will need a strong man around the farm now that I have no son."

"What about Cobus?" asked Hennie. "He will be back soon, I'm sure. He's still your son."

"He is no son of mine!" rasped Oom Jaco angrily. "He has raped, stolen and murdered. He has made his choices ... bad choices. Last night he gave up any right to be called my son."

Oom Jaco looked at Hennie, his hand still on the young man's shoulder.

"I fear your cousin has been a bad influence on you, boy. We will have to change that."

Chapter 14

2010

Thuli came around from her faint to find Detective Malepo cradling her head on his knees. Her first thought was that he was incredibly good-looking, in a brash Hollywood cop way. But then she remembered what he had just told her, and the horror returned.

"Oh my God," she moaned. "Why is this happening to me?"

Malepo frowned at her, his favourable first impressions evaporating.

"Actually, in comparison to the victim, you're doing pretty well," he answered crisply, standing up and letting her head drop to the floor with a thump.

Thuli stood up, fingering the bump that was already forming where her head had made contact with the black-and-white tiles.

"Now," he repeated his earlier question, "do you have somewhere you can go for a couple of weeks?"

"I'll go and stay with my grandmother in the location," said Thuli.

After making a note of both Gogo and Julie van Tonder's addresses, Jack accompanied Thuli upstairs to pack.

"I'm able to pack my own suitcase without your help, thank you," she said tartly.

"I'm sure you are, but this is now a crime scene, and I can't have you wandering around and contaminating the evidence, even if it's decades old."

Furious, she slammed her bedroom door in his face and threw clothes at random into a suitcase. She then went through to the bathroom and collected her toiletries, and from there into her study for her laptop and some papers. Eventually she was ready, and Malepo followed her down the stairs.

Thuli heard her grandmother's voice, questioning Julie. It never failed to amaze her how her grandmother always knew what was happening before anyone else, and managed to turn up where she was most needed. Julie, oblivious to everything and everyone, was sitting on the sofa staring into space. Thuli was worried about how badly Julie was taking the situation.

"This is a bad story, Thuli," said her grandmother with a shake of her head. "You're coming home with me."

"I'm pleased to hear that," said Thuli with a sulky look at Jack Malepo, "because I'm being turned out of my house."

Taking Julie's arm, Thuli followed her grandmother out to her car.

Jack Malepo had watched admiringly as Thuli marched indignantly down the garden path, flanked by her grandmother and Julie van Tonder. Just my type, I'd like to get to know that one a bit better, he thought. Then he shook his head sadly, fat chance of that with a potential murder to investigate. The boss would have something to say if he started fraternising with the witnesses.

He sighed regretfully and turned back to the garage. Careful not to scuff his expensive and highly polished shoes, he carefully climbed through the small gap the builder had made while trying to find the old laundry.

He turned on his flashlight and shone the light around the tiny room, which picked up the skeletal figure lying on its side next to what appeared to be an ancient twin-tub washing machine. There were no clothes on the body that he could see, but those might have disintegrated over the years.

His light caught a wire that surrounded the skeleton's left wrist, with a chain that attached it to a bar on the wall.

There was a lot of rubble lying around, and the flickering light cast menacing shadows on the walls. Long-dead spiders had spun webs that trailed along the walls and down from the ceiling. It felt like something out of a B-movie.

Jack had investigated many murders during his time on the force, but this was completely different to anything he had seen before – firstly, because this was obviously a very old murder, and secondly, because he seemed to be in some sort of time capsule from about half a century ago.

He checked his watch. Surely the crime-scene people should be here by now? Then he heard the sound of approaching voices.

Jack recognised the distinctive voice of the doctor, Henry Morgan. He smiled to himself, trying to imagine the doctor manoeuvring his ample frame through the small aperture. He guessed he would not make it, and was right. The doctor took one look at the hole in the wall and demanded loudly that it be enlarged. The next face Jack saw was the lean face of his partner, Joe Bantu. His teeth gleamed white in his dark face.

"Hello, my brother," he said as he saw Jack. "I hear you have an interesting one for us here."

"You can say that again!" answered Jack. "It's like nothing I've ever seen before."

Jack shone the beam of his torch steadily onto the remains while Joe moved around with the grace of a ballerina, taking photographs not only of the skeleton but also of the surrounding area.

"What's going on in there?" boomed Doctor Morgan's voice.

"I think we can break the hole bigger," answered Joe. "We must just be careful to prevent the bricks from falling into the room."

"Can you do that?" Doctor Morgan asked the builder.

"Sure, no problem."

Soon they were covered in dust as the builder used his hammer and chisel to remove more bricks. As the hole got bigger, so the light improved.

After having a thorough look around, Jack left them to it, instructing Joe to call him if anything interesting turned up. Until he had some idea of when the skeleton had met its end, he could not really start investigating. He needed to start doing a bit of digging of his own, starting with the ownership of the house before Thuli Nyembe bought it.

The builder had said something about the house belonging to the Van Tonders before Thuli bought it. He needed to find out more about that.

Jack decided to have a chat with Mrs van Tonder first. Perhaps she would be able to throw some light onto the mystery.

Julie was in no state to drive, so Thuli took her home and encouraged her to rest for an hour or two so that she could recover from her shock.

The sound of the doorbell woke Julie from a deep and troubled sleep, and she almost fell out of bed in her haste to answer it. She opened the door to find Detective Jack Malepo on her doorstep.

"Sorry to trouble you, Mma," he said politely. "I wonder if you could help me to answer a few questions that are buzzing around in my head."

Julie opened the door wider, and Jack followed her in, stopping in the hallway to admire a large framed wedding photograph of Katie and Patrick.

"Is this your daughter?" he asked.

"Yes. She got married recently and has gone to live in England."

"That's Patrick Tshabalala. I remember him well," he smiled. "We occasionally played football against each other when we were boys. I was always worried when I saw his name on the line-up. It was a sure sign that we were going to lose the game."

"He plays for Chelsea in England now," smiled Julie proudly, relaxing in the charm of his manner.

"Yes, I know. I've been following his progress. He's a bit of a hero around here. Local boy makes good. And a lucky man too, your daughter is very beautiful."

Julie beamed at him. Obviously, he was a man with excellent taste. She offered Malepo a cup of tea, which he accepted. In his experience, the making and drinking of tea was a good way of getting people to relax, and he sat patiently until Julie returned with the tray.

He waited until she had taken a few sips before commencing.

"Miss Thuli said that she only recently bought that house. Do you, by any chance, know who it belonged to before?"

"Yes. It belonged to my husband's father."

"Do you have any idea when he bought it?

"No, not really. I do know that they lived in that house for a long time."

"Is your father-in-law still alive?"

"Oh yes," answered Julie. "He lives at the retirement home across town. Woodlands. He has been there almost a year, since he broke his hip."

"Is he well enough to talk to me, do you think?"

"I think so. I have only seen him once since he moved there. To be honest, he is a miserable old man, and I always left the care of him to my husband. Rick is the only person in the world he seems to like."

"What time does your husband get home?" asked Malepo.

"Oh, I am sorry. I didn't mean to give you the wrong idea," replied Julie, her face darkening. "My husband had a bad stroke about a month after his father went to live at Woodlands. He also lives at the retirement home now."

"Really? That is very convenient for me. I will be able to kill two birds with one stone and speak to both of them there."

"I doubt you'll have much luck with my husband," Julie said quietly. "His stroke left him unable to speak. I think he can understand what people are saying but just can't communicate."

"Hmm, that'll certainly complicate things. Maybe I'll have more luck with your father-in-law then."

He saw himself out, leaving Julie to wonder what part, if any, either her husband or her father-in-law had played in the death of the person whose skeleton had been found in Thuli's house. As much as she hated the idea, it would not surprise her if the old man was implicated in some way.

Chapter 15

1939

The repercussions of those two terrible days were enormous for everyone on the farm.

Robbed of their right to a life for their chief's life, the workers left the farm overnight, taking their possessions and livestock with them.

There were plenty of farmers looking for reliable workers, and it was almost six months before Oom Jaco managed to find a few layabouts who were prepared to come and work on his farm for the pittance he could now afford to pay.

Oom Jaco and Hennie spent all the hours of the day simply keeping up with the basic work, and when the new workers arrived, their work needed to be constantly supervised. Oom Jaco seemed to age rapidly, while Tant Sarie was even quieter than before, her hair turning snow white.

About a year after Cobus left, Hennie returned from the milking shed to find Oom Jaco waiting for him, dressed in his Nagmaal suit. He sent Hennie off to hitch up the cart, and presently he was riding off towards Standerton. In all of Hennie's years on the farm, Oom Jaco had never gone into town, except for Nagmaal.

Hennie stood for a long time, watching the cart disappear into the distance. He walked slowly back to the farmhouse to find Tant Sarie crying on the stoep.

"Where has Oom gone?" he asked.

"He has gone to disown Cobus," said Tant Sarie through her tears. "He has gone to see the lawyer to make a new will, disinheriting his own son, his own flesh and blood."

Whatever his crime, Cobus was still her son, her firstborn, and she loved him fiercely. She had fought for many months, trying to change Oom Jaco's mind. But he was adamant that Cobus had forfeited his right to be called their son, and if Oom Jaco had any say in the matter, Cobus would never set foot on the farm again. As far as he was concerned, Cobus was dead to the family.

The sun was already setting when Oom Jaco returned, looking grim but satisfied. He carried with him a new strongbox and a sheaf of papers, which he placed into the new box, together with the Bible and the other family papers. The box was then bolted firmly to the floor. Oom Jaco was not taking more chances.

Oom Jaco and Tant Sarie sat together on the stoep; her chair a rustic stool; his, an ancient rocking chair which creaked mournfully with every movement. Hennie sat on the step watching the last of the autumn light fade from the sky.

Tant Sarie did not ask the question and Oom Jaco did not answer. He had done what he had set out to do, and had the papers that made his decision final.

"The country is at war," he said presently.

"War?" asked Hennie. "Against whom?"

"Germany!" answered Oom Jaco.

"Why Germany?" asked Hennie, interested. "They are our friends, aren't they?"

"They may be our friends, but they're not friends of the cursed English who rule this country now!"

Like many Afrikaners, Oom Jaco hated the British. He had heard many stories about the Boer War from his father who had fought in it, how the British had come to steal the land that God had given to His chosen people.

The superior British forces had won, and the Boer farmers had eventually returned to their land; beaten but not bowed; turning their backs on their new government; fiercely independent and acknowledging no one but God's authority and their own. Hennie had also heard the stories, and he hated them too. In his naiveté, and although he had never met a single Englishman, his hatred had strengthened and clarified with each new tale of tyranny; real or fictional.

"They are trying to make our boys go to war against the Germans," laughed Oom Jaco sourly. "As if they could find a single farmer's son who would fight on their side."

"I would go and fight against the British!" exclaimed Hennie.

"You will do no such thing!" snapped Tant Sarie angrily, determined not to lose him as well.

"I am old enough!" said Hennie defensively. "I am nineteen; definitely old enough to fight."

"Your place is here with me, tending the farm," said his uncle firmly. "Do you have any idea where Germany is?"

"No. Is it far?" asked Hennie. He had never travelled further than Standerton, fifteen kilometres away.

"If you took the fastest horse," laughed Oom Jaco sourly, "it would take you three weeks to reach Durban and the sea. Then you would have to catch a big ship to take you on a journey lasting another four months before you reached Germany. By the time you got there, the war would be over, and the British would have lost without any of your help!"

Hennie pondered his uncle's words for some time. The idea of seeing the sea was an adventure he would love to experience. He tried to imagine what the sea could be like. And what about being on a ship? He imagined something like a big canoe, with strong young men rowing for four months across a large expanse of dark water. That thought was less appealing.

Hennie had been feeling restless for some time. With Cobus gone, he was working from sunrise to sunset seven days a week, without respite. Even Nagmaal had lost its appeal as he was unlikely to be able to find a wife. He had no home to bring her to, and no inheritance. He mooched sullenly around the edges of the jolly crowd and ended up in a bar drinking brandy with a few other similarly placed young men; men without prospects and without a future.

Inevitably, the conversation turned to the war which was raging thousands of kilometres away, between two countries of which they knew very little. This did not prevent them from having strong opinions and boasting about what they would do to any Rooinek reckless enough to cross their paths.

As their evening had been fuelled by several bottles of sweet cherry brandy, their conversation was clearly audible to the other men sitting close to them in the bar.

"So, you heroes want to fight the British?" Hennie turned to the stocky, dark-haired young man of about thirty who was standing next to him. He had a dark beard and vivid blue eyes under heavy brows.

Brave with the copious amounts of alcohol they had consumed, the young men all expressed a strong desire to fight the British and flush them all out of their beloved fatherland.

"Well, if any of you still feel this way when you sober up tomorrow morning, meet me behind the church at sunset. Bring a horse if you have one, and your clothes. And say goodbye to any sweethearts you may have met." He gave a sudden smile, his eyes crinkling at the corners, and the boys were hooked. This charismatic man was offering them the adventure they were craving.

The rest of the evening was spent describing in exquisite detail what they would do to any Rooinek, if they got the chance to fight the English.

Chapter 16

2010

The next morning, after spending a few hours at the office going through some old files and trying to find anything that might have a bearing on the case, Jack Malepo stopped off at the mortuary. Doctor Morgan was not an expert on bones and had called in a colleague from Johannesburg to assist in trying to pinpoint the time of death. His estimate was somewhere between forty to fifty years ago based as much on the contents of the bricked in laundry as the evidence from the bones.

Jack was told that the victim was definitely a woman, and from her facial bone structure they could tell she had been a black woman. Doctor Morgan estimated her to have been in her mid-thirties at the time of death.

Without the exact date of death, other than somewhere between 1960 and 1970, Jack had no baseline from which to search the records for a woman who might have been reported missing during that time. So her identity remained a mystery.

Jack decided to pay a visit to the council offices to see if he could find out who had owned the house during that time. His first obstacle was that the computerised records only went back as far as 1984.

The young man from the property section at the council was leaning back in his chair, dreadlocks caught back in a green and yellow scarf, his iPod earphones thumping out music which was loud enough for Jack to hear from across the room. His first thought was that the guy would be deaf by the time he was thirty.

The name on the counter said Harry Tsotsetsi. Getting Harry's attention from across the counter was Jack's second problem. He first tried ringing the service bell. Then he called Harry's name. Finally, he resorted to picking up a form from the counter, rolling it into a ball, and throwing it at the guy.

Harry was inclined to be belligerent at having paper thrown at him, until he saw Jack's badge. He still managed to be sullenly unhelpful, and it was only when Jack's frustration boiled over into a quiet but threatening description of what would happen to Harry if he did not cooperate with the police that he finally agreed to go through the archives and locate the records for the house. He made it sound like a big favour, offering to have the information available within a week.

Jack had thus far managed to control his frustration, but now he had had enough. He leaned across the counter and held Harry's eyes menacingly.

"I want it in three days tops, so get your thumb out, now!"

As Jack climbed back into his car he heard his phone bleep, indicating an incoming message.

It simply said, "Call Joe immediately."

He dialled the number and waited to hear Joe's voice.

"Jack, you need to come to the house straight away. There has been a serious development. This is a bad scene, man."

He was back at the house a short while later. Joe was standing outside, surrounded by six crime-scene officers in white overalls and masks.

"What's up?" he asked, astonished at the sudden increase in activity at what was really a very old, and therefore not very urgent, crime scene.

"You'll need to see this for yourself," said Joe gravely, leading the way back to the garage. Jack followed his partner and found that Doctor Morgan was also back at the scene.

Morgan looked up at him, a serious and sad expression on his face.

"Jack, you will have to look at this."

He led the way to a long cabinet in the corner of the room and lifted the top. Doctor Morgan angled his flashlight down into the cabinet. The light caught a skull, a very small skull.

Jack took the flashlight from Doctor Morgan's hand and concentrated the light onto the skull. It was too small to have come from an adult.

He sucked in his breath. He hated crimes that involved children, and this definitely was a child's skull. He played the light further into the cabinet and picked up more bones, and then another skull.

"Where are the lights, for fuck's sake!" he shouted. "Bring some lights and let's see properly what's in this room."

Within a few minutes there were more flashlights illuminating the contents of the cabinet.

Jack felt his stomach churn. All the bones he could see were small and delicate. They were children's bones, and he could count at least four skulls. What kind of evil was this?

Jack had never vomited at a crime scene before, but he could feel his stomach churning. Passing the flashlight back to the doctor, he made his way hurriedly outside into the light and fresh air. He leaned over a flower planter on the patio and took some deep breaths, calming his breathing and bringing his heaving stomach under control.

Joe came out and stood patiently while Jack recovered from his horror.

"You okay?" he asked eventually. Jack nodded wordlessly and sat down on one of the patio chairs.

"I want that room opened up properly, and floodlights installed. Then I want the whole room photographed, every inch of it. After that, I want the bones removed and taken to the mortuary, ready for the arrival of the bone expert tomorrow morning.

"In the meantime, I want you to find out about the décor of that room. I want to know what year that old washing machine was manufactured and the age of all that equipment down there. That should give us some sort of timeframe for this crime.

"Also, see if there are any personal effects – clothes, anything – with the skeletons, and bring them down to the station."

Joe nodded, happy in the knowledge that he had started the ball rolling on most of those requests already.

"Now, I need to talk to Doctor Morgan."

Jack went through to the kitchen where Doctor Morgan was sitting with a cup of coffee and a pile of biscuits.

"Have a biscuit," offered the doctor.

Jack declined politely, but accepted the offer of a cup of coffee – black, strong and sweet.

"Tell me, doctor, am I right in thinking those are children's skulls?

"No doubt about that," nodded the doctor.

"Black children, like the other skeleton?"

"It certainly looks like it, though I will wait for my colleague from Johannesburg to confirm that."

"Jesus," he muttered in horror, "there must be at least four children there. It's a bloody massacre. How, why, when? And who?"

"Actually, looking at the skeletons, I would guess that there are more than four, though we will have to wait to get them all out. I will give you the full report as soon as I have them at the mortuary."

Jack needed to clear his mind. He drove his car down to the bank of the Vaal River and went to sit on a wooden bench overlooking the swiftly flowing water which was surrounded by weeping willow trees. The sound of the running water, the breeze through the trees, and the songs of the birds were usually enough to restore his spirit when he felt frustrated or upset, and today he was both. He allowed his mind to drift.

It must have been pretty much the same as this, forty or fifty years ago, he thought. It must have been as beautiful, the sun as warm, the dragonflies as colourful and energetic. And yet dark and dreadful things had happened which were successfully covered up for generations.

It was normal in the early stages of an investigation to feel as if you were hitting a brick wall. However, you could usually follow the trail, and often succeed in finding the truth.

The problem here was that the trail was half a century old. How do you begin an investigation if you can't pinpoint where it actually began? And after so many years, was it even possible that the killer was still alive?

He sat for a while, pondering what he had seen and thinking of possible scenarios. Finally, he decided to go to the retirement home and speak to the Van Tonders. He had a feeling that they might have the answers to all these questions.

Chapter 17

As Jack arrived at the retirement home, his first thought was that there was a strange and musty smell in places where old people were gathered. He walked down the corridor, passed a line of wheelchairs facing a television set, the sound barely audible. It was a very dated American soap opera, probably from the eighties, judging by the cars and the women's hairstyles. Jack estimated that the occupants of the wheelchairs averaged around the age of ninety, bodies shrunken, hands crippled with arthritis; most of them totally oblivious to their surroundings and the activity going on around them.

He crossed himself and prayed that he would not live past seventy. This was not living. This was sitting in God's waiting room, waiting for your name to be called.

One old man seemed more aware than the others and watched Jack as he passed by. Jack had the feeling that there was a lot more than idle curiosity in the stare, and felt strangely uncomfortable. As he reached the matron's office, he turned around to find the old man still watching him.

His first stop was Rick van Tonder, who was lying in bed, apparently asleep. But he opened his eyes when he heard his name.

Jack introduced himself and showed his badge.

"I have just come from Miss Thuli Nyembe's house. Do you know it?"

There was no response from Van Tonder.

"This house was bought recently on auction. You were listed as the seller, although the house actually belonged to your father. Is that correct?"

Rick did not, and could not, reply. His eyes cried out in enquiry, perhaps confusion.

"Can you blink your eyes?" Jack asked.

Rick blinked his eyes.

"Well, that's progress," said Jack with some satisfaction. "Let's say one blink for yes and two blinks for no."

Rick blinked once.

"So, going back, the house was put on auction by you?"

One blink.

"And the house originally belonged to your father?"

One blink.

"How long did your father own the house?"

Nothing.

"My mistake, sorry. Umm... did your father own the house for more than thirty years?"

One blink.

"Did he own it for more than forty years?"

Nothing.

"Are you saying you don't know?"

One blink.

Rick van Tonder was staring intently at Jack.

"You will be wondering what this is all about, I dare say," he said, smiling.

One blink.

"Well, unfortunately, at this time I'm not in a position to tell you. What I can tell you is that the house is the subject of a murder investigation."

Rick continued to stare at Jack with intensity in his eyes.

"Would you know anything about a murder that might have taken place there, say, thirty to fifty years ago?"

Jack thought he saw confusion in Rick's eyes, and pressed his point.

"That was one blink for yes and two for no. Now, do you know anything about a murder that might have happened in that house thirty to fifty years ago?"

Two blinks.

"Hmm... Well, don't go anywhere!" he quipped, rather pleased with his tasteless joke. "I'll need to speak to you again."

Rick van Tonder glared at Jack as he sauntered out of the room.

Chapter 18

1940

In the end it was only Hannes Marais and Hennie who turned up behind the church.

Hennie had awoken beside the ashes of the fire with an aching head and the feeling that he had forgotten something. That something proved to be the horses he should have watered and fed the previous evening.

Hennie was sitting on a rock, nursing the fire back into flames and hoping to brew some coffee to clear his aching head, when Oom Jaco arrived, his face like thunder. Some things he could accept, but he could never condone the neglect of his animals.

Hennie heard all about his incompetence, his ingratitude for the kindness heaped on him, and other flaws in his character that he never even suspected he had. Oom Jaco's sjambok twitched in his hand and from long experience Hennie turned to run. But the alcohol he had consumed the previous night had slowed his reflexes. Oom Jaco's hand flashed as he grabbed Hennie's arm and brought his sjambok down on Hennie's back three, four, five times, splitting the skin and shredding his shirt. He felt the warmth of the blood as it splattered his back. Finally Oom Jaco was satisfied and left Hennie to collapse onto the grass.

His first thoughts were drowned out by the overwhelming feeling of pain. This was not the first time he had experienced the sjambok, though generally with better reason. On this occasion he felt that the punishment had been excessive, and he brooded angrily as he clutched his coffee mug between his bloody hands.

What Hennie did not know was that Oom Jaco had been approached during the Nagmaal by one of his creditors to pay off a debt that had been outstanding for some time. Since Cobus had made off with all of his funds, he was unable to meet the request. The shame of having to beg for an extension infuriated and embarrassed him. Hennie was unfortunate that he had provided the spark needed to trigger the fury that his uncle had been forced to control when dealing with his creditors.

The pain of his back and the after-effects of the alcohol did not improve Hennie's mood, and soon the horses were being treated to a tirade of his own as he slopped water into their trough and unpacked a roll of hay.

This done and his headache abating, he mulled over the words of the stranger in the bar. At first it seemed completely impractical to abandon his life and follow a total stranger into an unknown world, but the more he thought about his hard life, and about the beating and the venomous insults his uncle had heaped on him, the more attractive the prospect became.

His uncle obviously cared little for him. He deserved to be deserted by someone who was effectively little more than a slave. He received no wages, only meals, and still slept on a mattress on the floor of the stoep.

After Cobus left, the farm had become a lonely place, and the stranger at the bar had promised adventure, excitement and comradeship. Hennie felt he would be crazy to miss this chance. He sought out his drinking partners from the previous night, but only Hannes still showed an interest. At sunset, the two young men waited behind the church, clutching their horses' bridles in sweaty palms, their possessions slung in bundles over the pommels of their saddles. Their adventure was about to begin.

The sun had already sunk, and Hennie was beginning to fear that the strange dark man of the previous night had been a figment of their imagination. They listened for sounds of his approach, but all they could hear were the rustling sounds of nocturnal animals and the occasional hoot of an owl. Suddenly, they both heard it – the sound of quiet hooves on the ground. They turned to see a lone figure on a dark horse emerging from the shadows.

"Are you the only ones?" he asked. They nodded. "My name is Andries Stander. You are now under my command, and soldiers of the Ossewa Brandwag. Whatever I tell you to do you will do without question. That way you will stay alive, and live to fight the British. Now mount up and follow me."

It took four days of hard riding to reach the place outside Bloemfontein where the movement was based. They followed the old animal tracks, avoiding contact with anyone, skirting towns and farmhouses. By the time they arrived, they had been joined by eighteen other young men, twenty being the typical number of members in a troop.

The following six months were spent in intense training in a small valley surrounded on all sides by high hills. Few of the young men had fired a rifle before, and they spent hours shooting at targets until they were able to hit a mosquito off a branch. They also learned how to work with explosives, and spent many hours listening to older men rail against people like Jan Smuts and Louis Botha, who had fought against the British and then turned their coats to join forces with the same British forces when the Boers were defeated.

This was an exciting time for Hennie. There were many firsts. He received his first new clothes, a set of brown fatigues and a suede hat – a symbol of his new status as a member of the Stormjaers, the military wing of the Ossewa Brandwag.

As he was able to read and write, Hennie spent many hours reading the newspapers that came his way, often reading aloud to his mostly illiterate comrades. He had never seen newspapers before and loved reading about what was happening in the country, as well as further afield.

He received his first pay; actual money to spend on whatever took his fancy. And for the first time in his life, he saw trucks and motor cars from close up.

One such car was driven by a fair young man, but it was the figure in the back that caught his attention. He had seen pictures in the newspaper of the man, Hans van Rensburg, the leader of their movement.

He had heard that Van Rensburg would be speaking in the training ground and hurried to be at the front of the crowd. Suddenly, his eye caught a familiar profile. Could that possibly be Cobus opening Van Rensburg's door, a black peak cap under his arm, body straight and proud?

He called out Cobus's name. Only by a brief movement of his eyes did Cobus acknowledge his cousin's shout. It was only after he had accompanied Van Rensburg to the platform from which he was to address the crowd that Cobus went in search of his now grown-up younger cousin.

There was much hugging, punching and talking, and Hennie found that he was no longer interested in hearing his hero speak. He much preferred to be with Cobus.

The subject of Cobus's departure and the events that led up to it were not discussed, not then. Those wounds ran too deep to be brought into the open here, surrounded by relative strangers.

"How did you come to be General van Rensburg's driver?" demanded Hennie eagerly, "and when did you learn to drive a motor car?"

"I was in the right place at the right time. I heard the general speaking to a group of students at the university in Pretoria, and at the end of the rally I went up and offered to follow him wherever he was going. He said he liked my spirit, and I have been with him ever since."

"And the car? Aren't you scared to drive it?" asked Hennie admiringly.

"It's easier than it looks. Once you get it going, it's simple. You just point it in the direction you want to go."

The general was due to stay at the camp for the whole week, so Hennie and Cobus had plenty of opportunities to meet up later to catch up on news. Cobus was amazed at the transformation his cousin had made from child to man in just four years.

He looked Hennie over, clearly impressed.

"You have grown up into a man. How old are you now?"

"You know exactly how old I am. Twenty-two years. Four years younger than you."

"I can't believe my father let you come. How did you manage that?"

Hennie hung his head in shame.

"I didn't ask," he said ruefully. "We were in Standerton for the Nagmaal, and we got talking to our captain, Andries Stander. He offered us the chance to join up. I was upset about something, I forget what it was. So I just saddled my horse and rode out."

Cobus whistled, imagining his father's reaction at losing not one but both his helpers. The first flush of Cobus' anger had cooled within a week of his dramatic departure, and he was ashamed of stealing his father's money.

In his ignorance, he imagined that his father would have funds elsewhere and had not realised how much hardship he had caused the household. He also heard for the first time that the workers had walked out, leaving his father and Hennie without the means to earn any more money.

Listening to Hennie recount the hardship of recent years, Cobus's betrayal of both his father and Hennie seemed more serious than he had at first thought, and he felt a momentary pang of guilt. That was until he heard that his father had disowned and disinherited him. He could not believe that his father had taken this unprecedented step, and was furious. As the only son, he believed that the farm was his by right, and he had childishly assumed that all would soon be forgiven; that he would return like the prodigal son.

Nothing was said about the child who had died, or the old man with the spear through his heart. Some things were better left unsaid, though the images of both were like ghosts demanding to be acknowledged and avenged.

"And what about Nesta?" asked Cobus. "Is she enjoying being married?"

"I don't know," answered Hennie. "I saw her a couple of times at Nagmaal, but she acted like I didn't exist. She has become very proud and important since she married a rich man."

"She wasn't always so proud, was she?" laughed Cobus slyly. "We had a lot of fun with her, hey boet, you and me?"

Hennie laughed sheepishly, hiding his blushes and remembering Nesta's mocking laugh and waggling little finger. Some memories were better left buried.

Chapter 19

2010

It did not surprise Jack that Van Tonder was the old man who had watched him with such interest as he had passed the old folks in the television room earlier.

The nurse introduced Van Tonder, suggesting that they had something in common.

"What is that?" asked Jack.

"You are both police officers," said the nurse, "or a former police officer, in Mr van Tonder's case."

"Is that right?" Jack asked Van Tonder, who did not deign to reply.

"Actually, you will have more in common now," she laughed, "Mr van Tonder's granddaughter is married to Patrick Tshabalala."

Van Tonder glared at her.

"You know who he is, I am sure. Soon Umkhulu will have lovely little coloured great grandchildren."

This was obviously a big joke amongst the nurses because they all shook with laughter. Jack caught a swift look of fury that shadowed the old man's face, while his hands curled into fists.

Aha, thought Jack, storing that glance in his memory. It is pretty clear what he thinks about Katie marrying Patrick. Not a happy grandfather-in-law!

Jack showed Van Tonder his badge and asked how he was adjusting to his move to the retirement home. Van Tonder gave him a blank look and turned to face the television. Jack smiled to himself, thinking that he was about to be treated to the senile old man routine.

"So, you used to be a policeman," Jack said, apparently to himself. "I wonder what sort of crimes they had in your day. Nothing much, I should think. How did the average cop fill his time in those days?"

Van Tonder maintained the blank look.

"I have often wondered about the cops back then in the apartheid years. Did they enjoy the work they did? Rounding up innocent people without passes and throwing them into cells; beating up anyone who dared so much as look at them. You must all have felt like such heroes."

No response, but Jack picked up the movement in Van Tonder's jaw as he clenched his teeth.

"Well, these days the tables have turned, haven't they? These days, the kaffirs are in control." Jack watched as Van Tonder's shocked eyes swivelled for a moment then resumed to stare at the television.

"Look, this is getting boring, and I have a lot to do, so you can talk to me or we can go down to the station."

Involuntarily, Van Tonder turned to face Jack but quickly turned back.

"Oh, I think you would enjoy that," said Jack. "I think you are bored to death in this place and would enjoy a little field trip. Am I right?"

"What do you want?" answered Van Tonder aggressively.

"It speaks!" laughed Jack.

"What do you want? Why are you here? And what do you want with my son?" barked Van Tonder.

"Actually, I will be asking the questions, Van Tonder," answered Jack, pleased that he had finally got a reaction out of the old man.

"As for the field trip; sadly, we will have to postpone that. All I want to know is how long you have owned your house."

"I don't own a house."

"Don't play with me. You know I'm talking about your house in Charl Cilliers Street that you sold recently on auction."

Van Tonder gave him a long look before he answered, biding his time.

"I didn't sell the house. It was stolen from me and sold without my authority. Are you here to investigate that crime?"

Jack shook his head impatiently and repeated his question.

"How long did you own the house?"

"Thirty-six years."

"Thirty-six years," repeated Jack. "You know, of course, that this can be verified."

"You can check the title deed. The date of transfer was March 1974."

This was said with such absolute certainty that Jack was convinced that the old man was telling the truth. However, a niggling doubt persisted in his mind. He hoped that Harry Tsotsetsi at the council offices would come back with a response soon. He needed that information.

Chapter 20

Thuli was in a state of despair about her house. She had invested everything she had in the place and was totally miserable at the thought that she might lose her home and never get it back.

Once the crime was solved, if it ever was, would she get the house back, and how would she feel about living there if she did?

These thoughts swirled through her mind, keeping her awake at night. It was with difficulty that she concentrated on what her client was saying.

Then she heard a woman in the queue at the bank saying that they had discovered the skeletons of a woman and child at a house in the town. It was unlikely that there would be more than one case in the small community involving an unidentified skeleton. Could there be more than one skeleton in her house?

I need some answers, she thought determinedly, and as her client left her office, she turned the sign on her door to 'Closed'. She dug into her bag to find her purse, removed Jack Malepo's business card, and dialled his number.

"Malepo," he answered.

For some inexplicable reason, Thuli disconnected, dropping her phone onto her desk. She stared at it for a few moments, embarrassed at her reaction.

That was really stupid, she thought, smiling to herself. She dialled again.

"Malepo," she heard again.

"Can you hear me?" she said brightly, pretending to have had a bad connection. She would have been mortified if he knew the reason she had dropped the phone.

"Yes, who is this?"

"Oh, sorry. Thuli Nyembe speaking. I was wondering if I could speak to you about the house."

"What do you want to know?" he asked brusquely. "Unfortunately, it will not be possible for you to return for another few weeks, so you should continue to stay with your grandmother."

"Well, I understand that, but what's happening there? Have you found out anything about the woman the builder found in the garage?"

"We know that she was a black woman in her thirties, and that she died between forty and sixty years ago. Unfortunately, we don't know much more than that about her, but we're in the early stages."

"How on earth did she end up in that room?" asked Thuli.

"Well, at this stage you probably know as much about that as I do," he answered shortly.

He seemed to want to end the conversation, and Thuli quickly pre-empted him.

"I heard a rumour – you know how these things go – that the skeleton of a child has also been found. Is that true?"

Thuli could hear the explosion down the line.

"How do these stories get around?" demanded Jack angrily.

"So, it's not true?" asked Thuli hopefully.

"I can't comment on that," snapped Jack, "and I suggest neither do you."

Thuli's stomach turned. The denial confirmed it. It was true. Not only was there a woman's body, there was also a child's body, in her house.

She looked at her watch. One hour to go and she could go home. She really needed the comfort of her Gogo's arms today.

Chapter 21

Jack snapped his phone shut and glared at the traffic light. *If I catch the idiot who leaked this to the public, I will make him sorry he was born.*

I suppose I was a bit hard on the woman, he thought. *It is not her fault that she heard the information, and at least she came to me for confirmation rather than just blurting it out to everyone. It must be hard for her, being turned out of her house like this.*

He decided to make amends.

As Thuli arrived at Gogo's house in the location later that afternoon, she found Malepo's car parked in the driveway. She overcame her irritation at finding someone parked in her space, and smiled as he climbed out of the car.

"Detective Malepo," she said with an ironic smile. "I didn't expect to see you here, so soon after being told so firmly to mind my own business."

"I have come to apologise, Miss," he said, smiling and holding his hands up apologetically. Like most men, Jack found it hard to make an apology.

"Apology accepted, and please call me Thuli."

"Thuli, I have always liked that name," smiled Jack, and followed her into her grandmother's house.

It was a spacious and comfortable house, with a big stoep running all the way around it. The house was much larger than most of the others in the location. It had obviously housed a large family at one time. Framed photographs going back several generations covered the walls, recording the history of the Nyembe family.

Among others, Jack saw photos of a young Mma Nyembe outside a large industrial building, flanked by two other women. There were pictures of Thuli as a little girl, more of her growing up and of her graduation, surrounded by a loving family. These days it was only the two of them, and Jack got the feeling that the old woman would be finding it very lonely here, now that Thuli had moved out. She must be enjoying having Thuli back in the house with her, despite the reason for her sudden return.

Gogo welcomed Jack. She had taken an instant liking to the handsome policeman, and had immediately identified him as a potential match for Thuli.

They sat down on the stoep, overlooking the noisy dusty street, full of people on foot coming home from work; vendors on the pavements selling cooked eggs, roasted mealies and soap, barbers in makeshift barbershops with clients sitting on upturned paint tins, housewives gossiping over the fences, children playing, and lean dogs running between them all. Cars had to carefully manoeuvre between the pedestrian traffic, the occasional hoot helping them on their way. Everywhere there was the sound of voices, laughter and music.

Thuli had tried to persuade Gogo to leave the location since the laws of the land had changed to allow people to live wherever they liked. But Gogo was adamant. She loved the constant noise of people coming and going, the activity, and the neighbours who had known her since she was a young woman. The suburbs were barren, as far as she was concerned. She belonged here, amongst her own people.

"Now, what do you have to tell us about Thuli's house and the unfortunate person who died there?" she asked gently.

"Well, actually Mma," he answered respectfully, "we've found more than one skeleton at the house."

Thuli looked at him with wide eyes. "So, what I heard is true. There was more than one person who died there."

"Well, to be honest, at this stage we don't know whether the people actually died there. They could have died elsewhere and been brought to the house afterwards."

"And the other person is a child, right?" asked Thuli.

"Aish, a child!" echoed Gogo, shocked. "You say there's a body of a child there too?"

Jack did not want to disturb them too greatly, and just nodded.

Thuli and her grandmother stared at him in horror. Thuli felt tears start down her cheeks.

"What happened? Can you tell whether they died, or were killed?"

"As I said, it's early days yet. We'll need a full examination of the bones to try to establish that. We have an expert arriving from Johannesburg tomorrow morning to examine the bones, and we'll then know what we're dealing with."

"Do you know when they died?" asked Gogo quietly.

"That is another thing the expert will be able to tell us. In the meantime, we are sifting through all the evidence in that room to try to establish some sort of timeframe for this crime."

Gogo seemed to have shrunk into her chair, and Thuli was suddenly reminded that her grandmother was getting old. Life expectancy for black women of her generation was around sixty-five. Her grandmother was almost there already.

Thuli brought a rug from the sitting room and wrapped it around her grandmother's shoulders.

"Come inside, Gogo, the wind has picked up," she chided gently.

"I feel it. It is an evil wind," answered the old woman enigmatically, "it opens up graves and exposes the bones of the dead."

Chapter 22

1940

It was some eight months later that Hennie had his first opportunity to fight the British. Information had been received that troops destined for North Africa would be departing from Durban harbour in April. Captain Stander's Stormjaers, now fully trained and deadly, made their way to Durban in the back of a closed truck.

It was Hennie's first experience of riding in any sort of vehicle and he found it a singularly unpleasant experience. The canvas top of the truck smelled of dust and petrol, and smoke from the exhaust permeated the space at the back, which was filled with twenty hot, sweaty young men.

To his eternal embarrassment, he soon found himself vomiting his breakfast out the back of the truck. His only consolation was that almost every member of the troop experienced similar discomfort. It was a sorry bunch that finally arrived in Durban.

They had one day to acclimatise before beginning their assignment. Andries Stander kept a close eye on them to ensure that they would be in peak condition for the task, which involved half the group placing explosives in the dock from where the vessel was to set sail, and the other half – including Hennie – finding suitable sites in the vicinity of the harbour from which to pick off individual soldiers, preferably the officers, as they boarded the ship.

Hennie was shaking as he settled himself at the top of a tall building overlooking the harbour. Until now, he had only shot at targets, and occasionally birds and animals for the pot, and the thought of shooting a man was terrifying. Remembering his training, he cleared his mind and checked his line of sight. There was much fanfare around the ship. The sound of a brass band carried through to where Hennie lay, and a holiday crowd surged around the dock. Handkerchiefs waved above the crowd, and the people cheered the smartly kitted troops as they marched up the gangplank.

Hennie breathed in and then slowly out, focusing on the man standing at the top of the gangplank who was saluting the troops as they embarked. Slowly, he squeezed the trigger. The shot rang out loudly. Although it deafened him, it was inaudible to those on the dock, drowned out by the brass band and the noise of the crowd.

Only the troops boarding the ship and those closest to the seafront saw the body crumple slowly forward, catch briefly on the rail, and drop lifelessly into the sea. There followed a surge of terrified people pushing back into the group behind them, and a rush onto the ship as the embarking troops scrambled to safety. Hennie saw and heard nothing of this. He lay on his back, staring up at the clear blue sky, the noise of the crowd drowned out by the sound of the blood drumming in his ears.

From his mates in their chosen hideouts he heard three more shots ring out, followed by several more, and suddenly the crowd on the dock were running wildly for cover. At that moment, an explosion ripped the roof off the harbourmaster's office. The panic turned into a stampede.

Remembering their briefing, Hennie methodically took apart his rifle and dropped it into the leather bag which he slung over his shoulder. He joined the crowd running from the carnage on the dock, making his way back by a devious route to their base. Soon the others joined him. All of them had made it safely into and out of battle. There was much whooping and laughing as they celebrated their first successful raid.

They weren't given much time to enjoy thmeselves. Captain Stander quickly restored order.

"We need to get moving fast," he said. "They'll be out looking for us within the hour."

Quickly, they climbed into the truck. This time there was no car sickness. The excitement had drained them all, and soon they were asleep, propped up against one another and oblivious to the kilometres flying by.

On their return to the camp they were hailed as heroes. The attack had caught everyone by surprise, and the losses were damaging to the morale of the South African troops. General van Rensburg came to congratulate them personally, driven as usual by Cobus. Hennie spent hours reading the reports in the newspapers. He carefully cut out the articles to place in his diary.

Cobus hugged and congratulated Hennie, hiding his envy of his cousin's achievement. Although driving the general was a prestigious job, it was not as exciting as being the hero of a major raid. Hennie had a new swagger to his walk and a more confident way of talking. Gone was the hero worship that had once shone in his cousin's eyes. Hennie had made it on his own. Cobus felt the change, and it galled him.

Chapter 23

As pleased as they were with their achievements, Captain Stander's men had only just started their reign of terror. They followed their success in Durban with raids on a railway station in Johannesburg, a barracks in Pretoria, and a fuel depot in Durban. South African soldiers who were originally destined for the war found themselves reassigned to protecting strategic industries and supply routes.

The leaders of the movement were elated with their achievements, and the small troop became celebrities among the three hundred and fifty thousand members of the Ossewa Brandwag, a group that included not only people willing to fight to achieve their goals, but ordinary Afrikaner folk of the town and the country. Their members included men, women and children from all walks of life – members of parliament; members of the clergy; senior advocates; doctors; simple farmers; shopkeepers; and schoolchildren. Their unifying ambition was the routing and removal of the British influence over the government in South Africa.

For three years, Hennie enjoyed his life in the Stormjaers. He enjoyed the excitement, the danger and the camaraderie of his fellow soldiers.

But this situation could not last forever. Long before the war ended, with the British celebrating their victory and troops returning from the front, a subtle change occurred. Ministers originally in favour of the movement started voicing their concerns about the violent nature of the Stormjaers. The popular support they had seemed to dissipate as though it had never existed. The heroes became an embarrassment. Those that could, disappeared back into country life, while the leaders were arrested and interned.

Finding that they no longer had any role to play was a hard reality for Hennie to accept. Hannes returned home to take over the family farm, following his father's death.

Hennie dreaded leaving the Stormjaers and returning to civilian life, but he had no other alternative. He headed back to Standerton, the only place he knew.

Unexpectedly, he found himself hailed as a local hero. Within days of arriving and before he had even decided what he was going to do with the rest of his life, he was offered several jobs. These ranged from respectable honest work to some which he believed to be quite shady. In the end, he settled for the police force, and found the life suited him perfectly.

It was strange to be back in Standerton. His only real memories of the town were of a few days twice a year during Nagmaal. He considered visiting his uncle and aunt on the farm, but his memory of the circumstances of his departure kept him away.

One evening, as he was leaving the police station, he was surprised to see Oom Jaco standing across the road. It was obvious that the old man was waiting to see him. He dreaded the confrontation he was sure was to come.

Seeing Hennie standing uncertainly across the road, Oom Jaco raised his hat to acknowledge him. Hennie overcame his reluctance and went to greet him.

"Oom," he said. "I'm happy to see you are well."

"And you have grown into a man," answered his uncle. "We heard about your exploits over the past few years, and we're proud! We're proud that you're our son."

Hennie bent his head to hide the tears of shame and regret that glistened in his eyes.

"I'm sorry that I left the way I did," he said in a low voice. "I was wrong, and I left you without any help. That was the action of a weak man."

"That was the action of a boy," answered his uncle, and laid his hand on Hennie's shoulder.

"Tant Sarie and I would be happy if you could come by some time and visit us. We still live in the farmhouse, but have sold off half the farm to Nesta's husband. You remember Tertius Serfontein? He has done very well for himself. Four thousand head of cattle he farms on his lands. The wealthiest farmer in the Transvaal! Nesta did well for herself. She was always a clever little thing."

Hennie remembered Nesta well, and Tertius, the memory of their departure in the cart vivid in his mind. Nesta had looked small and vulnerable as she sat on the seat of the cart. Yet she had a look of determination that would not be denied.

Hennie did not mention Cobus. Nor did Oom Jaco bring up the subject of his son, or the events that had made the sale of half of the farm a necessity. It seemed as if his uncle had really written Cobus out of his life completely.

Chapter 24

2010

Jack arrived at the mortuary as they were closing up for the day. Doctor Morgan was about to climb into his old Mercedes.

"You aren't leaving, are you?" he demanded.

"You can bet your sweet life I am," answered the doctor happily. "It's my thirtieth wedding anniversary, and if I don't arrive home well before we are due to go out for a fancy dinner, I'm unlikely to celebrate my thirty-first."

"Before you go, Doctor, can you tell me about the bones? How many children did you find?"

Doctor Morgan reluctantly withdrew his key from the ignition and heaved his substantial frame out of the car.

"At this stage, with all the bones now more or less sorted, we have two women and seven children. The second woman was found below the bodies of the children. The cause of her death is easy to see – the side of her head was struck by something large and round, and in all likelihood would have caused her death.

"The children are more difficult. Several of them have broken bones. I have counted two children with broken ribs and two with broken arms. The biggest child skeleton – possibly the oldest child – has broken ribs, and also a blow to the head, which may have been the cause of death. At this stage it is not possible to tell whether the skeletons are male or female. I presume Doctor Henderson will be able to shed more light on that."

He looked quizzically at Jack. "Are you alright, my friend?" he asked.

Jack nodded wordlessly, and slapped the doctor on the back.

"You get off to your anniversary party," he said.

He watched the doctor steer his venerable old car out of the parking lot. Then he returned to the station, his mind in a whirl.

This wasn't a murder. It was a massacre! He looked around the office. There was no one to help him. One junior staff member was picking up her handbag to go home.

He checked his emails and received one from Jules in the forensics department. A quick survey of the room led them to believe that the room was sealed up some time after 1960. Doctor Morgan and Sheila Henderson has suggested a period between 1960 and 1970, so that confirmed it, though he would have liked to have a more definite date.

Jack headed to the archive room with the cabinet that contained the unsolved missing persons' files. He took down the first of at least twenty boxes that were covered in dust, and checked the dates on the side of the box. Slowly, he started to go through the files, one by one.

The one thing that struck him quite early on was that there were hardly any files for missing black people. What did that mean? Did they not go missing, or were their disappearances not reported?

Five hours and six cups of coffee later, he was none the wiser. Although there was the odd reported disappearance, the investigations seemed to have been dropped very quickly in the case of black people.

Jack could only find one report which seemed to have been filed within the estimated period. A teacher at a farm school was reported missing. Jack read through the report. Nothing much. Her husband had reported her missing. The officer investigating had decided that she had probably left her husband, and no further action had been deemed necessary. Jack flipped over the page and stopped in his tracks. The investigating officer was a J. J. Mostert. But, more to the point, it was signed off by a senior officer, a Captain H. van Tonder!

The coincidence seemed too unlikely. He made a note in his notebook. The date was 1964. That was ten years before Van Tonder claimed to have bought his house.

Jack needed that title deed! That young rasta, Harry Tsotsetsi, had better get him that information promptly. Perhaps a word with his boss would get him moving a little faster than his usual laid-back speed.

Chapter 25

Jack was at the mortuary waiting as Doctor Henderson arrived. He was expecting a man, but the doctor who walked through the door into the mortuary was definitely all woman.

Doctor Morgan looked up from the skeleton of the woman on the table. He came forward to give Doctor Henderson a hug.

"You're a sight for sore eyes," he said happily, and brought her forward to introduce her to Jack.

Jack was always a little shy in front of beautiful white women, a kickback to the days when it was unacceptable for a black man even to look at a white woman. He greeted her politely and asked where she and Doctor Morgan had met.

"Call me Sheila," she said with a smile.

"Actually, he is my godfather, if you can believe it," she laughed. "Uncle Henry was my father's best friend through medical school until my dad died when I was a teenager. He's been like a father to me ever since. I'd have been lost without him."

She smiled at Doctor Morgan as she pulled on her gloves and put on her white coat. In a few moments she had transformed herself from a pretty young woman into a serious professional.

The children's skeletons were laid out in some sort of order on a large table, some fairly intact, others just loose bones. She looked at the bones for a few minutes without touching any of them, then turned to the skeleton of the older woman.

"Well, here we have a female who was probably in her early forties, though she may have been younger – black women aged fast in those days." She looked apologetically at Jack.

"They had a hard life," he replied. "They did most of the manual labour, working the land, raising the children and keeping the household. It would have made any woman old before her time. I have read that the average life expectancy of a black woman in those days was fifty years."

"Hard to believe, nowadays," said Doctor Morgan.

"As you suggested, the obvious cause of death was a massive blow to the head from a large flat surface. There is also a broken shoulder, which might have occurred during or immediately after her death. There is no healing, and the bones were not exposed when the break occurred."

She moved the magnifying glass closer to the head injury.

"Can you bring me a scalpel and a glass slide please, Uncle Henry," she asked. She then proceeded to carefully lift something from the damaged skull and place it on the slide.

Slipping the slide under the microscope, she examined it carefully for a few minutes before looking up.

"This is a silica-based rock, quite common in this region. It looks like she was either hit with a rock, or fell and hit her head on one. Either way, a blow like this would almost certainly have been able to kill her, though perhaps not immediately."

Sheila turned back to the body and carefully examined the skull.

"There is also a jaw fracture on the right-hand side. It looks like she received a massive blow, probably from a left-handed person, and fell back hard onto a rock. There is some staining on the skull around the injury that looks like blood. This indicates that she lived for at least a short while after sustaining the blow, perhaps a few hours."

"Can you tell me anything else about her?" asked Jack.

"Well, as expected, there are signs that she did a lot of manual labour, probably in her youth. She had given birth to at least one child, and there are signs of arthritis in her feet and hands, which would have caused her a lot of pain."

Jack wrote a few lines in his notebook.

Sheila turned to the skeleton of the younger woman.

She took her time, carefully examining every inch of the bones, particularly the wire cuff around her wrist. Jack remained silent, though Doctor Morgan made the odd comment or suggestion.

Finally, Sheila turned to Jack.

"You have probably already been told that she was a young black woman, mid-thirties, and had not borne any children."

Jack nodded.

"Now you want me to tell you how she died." She shook her head, and looked again at the bones of the young woman.

"It is not possible to say with any degree of certainty. There are no obvious injuries that might have killed her, and her body is completely bare of any tissue that we might test.

"However, I can tell you that she appears to have broken the ulna of her left arm, at the wrist, almost certainly as a result of being restrained. You can see the wire cuff tied around her wrist, which would have been impossible for her to remove with one hand, though she seems to have made the attempt."

She indicated the thick wire, still attached to a chain and metal bar, which had been removed from the floor of the room. The wire showed the marks of the pliers that had tightened it many years ago.

"You can see that the bone was never set, but there is clear evidence of some regrowth after the break, meaning that she was alive for some time after she broke her arm. If I was to make a wild guess, and based on how she was found, I'd say that it was possible that she starved to death. But as I said, this is speculation based on what little evidence we have."

"You are saying that she was tied up and starved to death."

"That pretty much sums it up, I'm afraid. It would've been a long and painful death."

"What about the time of death?"

"I'm afraid that will take a little longer to establish. I'll need to take a sample of bone from each of the skeletons to establish the approximate, and I emphasise approximate, time of death. With skeletons as old as these, it'll be pretty tricky. You're more likely to pinpoint time of death by examining clothes and other items found with the bodies."

She turned to Jack.

"Was there anything found with the bodies?"

"There have been a few items collected, but I haven't had time to go through them yet."

"You'll find your best clues there," she said.

Finally, Sheila turned to the bones of the seven children.

"This is going to take some time, to make sure we have the bones sorted correctly. Looking at the skulls, though, there are seven children aged from about six to eleven years.

"The oldest child had severe wounds, including broken ribs, a crack to the skull, and a broken hand, which looks as if it was crushed by a boot or a rock. The other bones all show some sort of trauma, mostly broken ribs, two broken arms, one shattered in several places. It is obvious that someone attacked these children with some sort of stick or club."

Jack rocked back on his heels and sucked in his breath. He could still remember receiving the odd beating as a child, but nothing along these lines. He tried to imagine the kind of man – it must have surely been a man – who could inflict such wounds on small defenceless children. This must have been the work of a psychopath.

"Do you think this was a single event, or could it have happened over a period of time?" asked Jack.

"Judging from the bones, I'd say that the damage was all inflicted by a single weapon, probably during a single event. Of course, there's also the possibility that it might have been the same weapon used over and over again on several occasions."

Jack stood silent, trying to imagine the scene – a violent man laying into a group of small children with a big stick, or knobkierrie. Did he kill the older woman first, as she tried to protect the children? And how long did the younger woman live after the others had died? What sort of abuse was she subjected to by the monster who had beaten these children to death? Did she eventually pray for death?

Sheila placed a soft hand on his shoulder.

"Are you alright, Jack?" she asked kindly.

Tears were rolling down his face, and he sniffed, searching in his pocket for a tissue. She handed him some paper towel from a roller. He blew feebly, and wiped his eyes, embarrassed that this lovely woman had seen his weakness.

"I'm sorry," he muttered into the paper. "It always affects me when a child is hurt, and this is just the worst thing I've ever seen."

"It's good to see that despite the terrible things you see in your job you are still affected by the suffering of the victims. That surely makes you a better policeman, and keeps you human."

He smiled gratefully.

"When do you think we'll have an approximate time of death?"

"Samples were sent off yesterday, so we can expect an answer by Monday. I have asked them to give this job priority, even though it is a cold case. I believe these people have waited long enough for their killer to be brought to justice."

Chapter 26

1952

Hennie quickly settled into his new life in the police force. His years as part of the Stormjaers soon seemed like a distant memory, but the training he received there stood him in good stead later on.

Within a few years he was promoted to captain, and for the first time in his life he felt that he had a future. The past still haunted him from time to time, but life seemed full of promise.

Hennie was starting to feel at home in the town. Locals were already greeting him on the street and treating him like a favourite son. He started looking around for a wife, hoping to settle down. There was no shortage of suitable and enthusiastic young women, and he chose Henrietta Breytenbach, the sister of one of his police colleagues. Hettie was everything he hoped for in a wife. Besides being a lovely young woman, a great cook and a loving companion, she was also a woman of conviction and fiercely loyal. They soon had a small but comfortable home and a son.

In the summer of 1952 it all changed. It was a lovely day, the hot weather tempered by a gentle cool breeze. Hennie was looking forward to a walk along the Vaal River with his wife and his little son Hendrik. It was his favourite time of day; just him, Hettie and the boy, in the cool of the evening.

He was folding away his files, ready to go home when a message came through that there was someone who wanted to see him. He put down his pen and went through to the charge office.

He recognised the voice before he saw the face.

"... and he sat on his skinny arse on that stool, tugging on the teats, with not a drop coming out. He was the worst dairy boy ever. It was weeks before he could coax a drop of milk out of those udders!"

Hennie joined in the general laughter but could not explain his feeling of dismay at seeing Cobus, leaning against the duty officer's desk. After so many years his old playmate was barely recognisable. His sturdy figure had thickened considerably. He was smartly dressed, his dark hair slicked back, and he sported a small sculpted moustache like Clark Gable.

"Hello boetie," said Cobus with a broad smile. "Remember me?"

Once Hennie had recovered from the initial shock he was pleased to see Cobus. He gave him a big hug, but somehow the old camaraderie was missing.

There was a feeling of unease that Hennie could not account for.

Cobus seemed to have done well for himself and proudly showed off his expensive new car to his cousin. They went for a ride around town in the red Chevrolet Fleetline, hot off the production line and newly landed from America at Durban harbour.

If Hennie wondered what Cobus had been doing to accumulate enough money to buy such a flashy car or how he was earning his living, he did not mention it. In his mind he could still see the empty strongbox, and he remembered vividly the hardships that the family went through after Cobus left with the fruits of his father's labour. The old man's life savings would buy a few of life's luxuries, he thought cynically, but he doubted they would have stretched this far.

It was soon apparent that Oom Jaco's money had all been spent a long time ago. Cobus skimmed over his activities over the eight years since he and Hennie last saw each other. Whatever those activities were, they were lucrative enough for him to have bought the car, but were apparently now no longer viable. He appeared to have arrived in Standerton with empty pockets.

He had returned to his roots, hoping to get back into his father's good graces and reclaim his inheritance. He was destined to be disappointed. Furiously, he told Hennie about his visit to the farm.

He had driven up to the farmhouse in his shiny new car, to be greeted by a shotgun held firmly in the old man's unsteady hands. Smiling, and keeping up a stream of banter, Cobus climbed out of the car, his hands above his head in a sign of appeasement. He was stopped in his tracks by a shot fired over his head – a warning to trespassers. He quickly got back into his car, and as he roared out in a cloud of dust, he glimpsed his mother's figure through the door, hiding in the shadows. Even she was not prepared to welcome home the prodigal son.

It seemed the right thing to do, to take his cousin home to meet Hettie and little Hendrik. At first the visit seemed to go well, and Hettie was happy that Hennie had brought his cousin to meet the family.

Cobus oiled his way into the house with his smooth charm and was soon amusing Hettie with his stories of their childhood, exaggerating some of them for effect.

Hennie's offer of a beer was rejected.

"I'm a brandy man, boet. But don't worry, I always carry a bottle or two in the car for emergencies."

The meal was barely over before things turned sour. Cobus's slimy charm disappeared after a few glasses of brandy. He lounged untidily on their sofa, smiling lecherously at Hettie and making suggestive comments. Eventually, he turned back to Hennie, who was sitting on the edge of his seat, flushed with anxiety.

"So boetie, you are a big deal these days. All the boys at the station were singing your praises. You have come a long way from being the stray dog that was dumped on my family because no one wanted him. If it wasn't for me, you would have died on that farm. You owe me big time, boet."

"And what exactly do I owe you?" asked Hennie quietly.

"Return of the hospitality we showed you, at the very least," answered Cobus with a wide wave around the house.

Hennie was further angered by the implications of these words and gesture. He was also uneasy about the way Cobus was watching Hettie. Under normal circumstances he would have shown the man the door. Yet his old devotion made him hesitate. Hettie, however, had no such qualms.

She marched through to the kitchen and beckoned Hennie to follow her. "I know he is your cousin, Hennie," she whispered furiously, "but that man is not staying in my house!"

Hennie nodded his agreement, searching for a solution.

"Phone the Phoenix Hotel and book a room in his name," Hennie said quietly, "then go up to bed, lock yourself and Hendrik in and leave the rest to me."

It was not easy, but eventually Hennie convinced Cobus to leave. Cobus laughed off the rejection, but Hennie had no doubt that sooner or later Cobus would make him pay for it.

He was surprised the following day when Cobus arrived at the station, full of remorse for his bad behaviour of the previous night. His charm was back, and before Hennie realised what he was doing, he had agreed to recommend Cobus for a job on the police force. As soon as Cobus left the offices he regretted his promise and tried to withdraw his offer but Cobus would not be deflected. He was relentless. Eventually Hennie gave in. Within a few months, Cobus had joined the police force as a junior constable.

The veneer of charm was thin, and very little of it was wasted on his cousin - except where it served his purpose. While other officers saw a convivial fellow officer, Hennie saw the violent young thug he had known in his youth.

It was a difficult situation for Hennie. Cobus took every opportunity to try to undermine him at work. Hennie was a popular officer with a good reputation for fairness to both his colleagues and the public, but there were always a few malcontents happy to side with his cousin.

Despite the support from his family, friends and colleagues, Hennie found the constant battle stressful, and became more and more distant, not only at work, but also with his family.

As the years went by, Cobus was constantly in trouble; violent and abusive to his colleagues and the public; insubordinate and aggressive to Hennie and his other superiors.

On many occasions, Hennie compromised his own principles to bail Cobus out of trouble. He knew that Cobus was effectively blackmailing him but did not know how to escape his influence.

Another thing was bothering him. Cobus was living far more lavishly than his income would have allowed, and Hennie suspected him to be involved in illegal activities. Cobus denied these accusations with a great show of innocence, and for old times sake, Hennie gave him the benefit of the doubt.

Chapter 27

It seemed to Jack that a return visit to the retirement home was indicated. It was a waste of time trying to extract anything from Rick van Tonder, but he was keen to talk to the old man again. Despite his initial unwillingness to help, the man intrigued him. Even though he had bought the house after the critical date, he was of that same vintage. He therefore may have information that could shed some light on the case.

Van Tonder was in what Jack deemed to be his normal morose mood, yet he was not unwilling to chat. Jack suspected that the old man was dying to know what was happening. He considered keeping him guessing for a while longer.

"So, I've been honoured with another visit from the police!" Van Tonder said sarcastically. "To what do I owe this honour?"

They were sitting out on the stoep. Several old men and women were seated in a line which stretched to the left and right of them. Jack would have preferred to speak without an audience, but judging from the vacant expressions on their faces, none of the residents were actually able to hear or make any sense of their conversation.

"I'm investigating an old murder."

"What does that have to do with me?" demanded Van Tonder.

"The bones were found in your house."

"I don't have a house," snapped the old man.

"Don't give me that bullshit. You know that I'm talking about your house that your son sold on your behalf on auction last year."

"When is this murder supposed to have taken place?"

"About forty to forty-five years ago, around 1965 say," said Jack.

Van Tonder gave Jack a sharp look. "1965, you say?" he asked thoughtfully. Jack saw a flicker pass over the old man's face, but then it was gone. He shook his head with a sour smile.

"I suppose that's why you asked me when I bought the house," he said sarcastically. "If you remember, I told you I got it in 1974. That means any murder that took place in that house occurred long before I owned it."

Suddenly, Van Tonder started to laugh, a wheezing hacking laugh that caught Jack by surprise.

"The new owner must be so pissed! He finds out his house is the scene of a crime. That'll be sure to bring down the value of the place."

"The new owner is a woman, Thuli Nyembe. She is obviously very distressed and has had to move out until the case has been resolved."

"Thuli Nyembe?" the old man repeated involuntarily, his eyes widening.

"Do you know her?" asked Jack.

"Never heard of her," Van Tonder replied dismissively, looking out at the garden.

Jack was sure he was lying but decided to let it pass for the moment.

"Did you know the previous owner of the house?" asked Jack.

"Before me, you mean? Do you ever really know the owner of a house you are buying?" he answered evasively. "Generally, these things are handled by estate agents, and the buyer and seller seldom meet."

"Well, if you remember anything relevant, please call me."

A memory was niggling Jack. He headed back to his office to look at the files he had been going through the previous night. Eventually, he found what he was looking for. Josephine Vilikazi was reported missing by her husband, Hector, in December 1964. She was a school teacher at a local farm school, forty-seven years old, and the mother of two teenage children, Evaline and Agnes.

She had gone on an outing with the school children and had not returned. Van Tonder was the senior officer in charge of the investigation. The report stated that she and her husband had often fought and that she had probably left him. Case closed.

The police did not seem to have spent more than half an hour investigating. Having met Van Tonder, Jack was not surprised. The old man did not have much time for people of colour and had probably simply gone through the motions.

Jack leaned back in his chair. Josephine was a school teacher and around the right sort of age. Was it possible that someone had attacked a class of children and that Josephine was killed in the process?

He made a note of the names in the file on his big chalkboard and asked Joe to try to locate a member of the family. Perhaps there was someone who remembered the disappearance of Josephine.

It was with renewed purpose that Jack returned to the council offices. He was ready for a fight if Harry Tsotsetsi had not found the information he was waiting for.

He marched into the office, ripe for a confrontation, if only to relieve his frustration. The wind was taken out of his sails when Harry flashed him a huge smile, big white teeth in a dark face.

"Hey, my brother, great timing! I was just about to phone you. Look what I found. It's the title deed of that property you asked me to look for."

He held the file coyly to his chest, just out of Jack's reach, but seeing the expression on Jack's face, he quickly handed it over.

Jack flipped open the file and the date leapt out at him. Van Tonder had bought the house in 1974! The old bastard had told the truth.

He paged backwards and forwards but there was no mistake. Jack could not believe his eyes. There must be some error, he thought to himself. He had been so sure that it was the old man. Yet here was proof that he had only bought the house ten years after Josephine had disappeared.

He almost threw the file on the desk.

"I would like a copy of this, please," he said politely, though he was itching to smash his fist through Harry's big white smile. No one deserved to look that pleased with himself whilst delivering such bad news.

Jack seemed to have exhausted all the leads of his investigation. He was boiling with frustration. Everyone was heading home for the beginning of the weekend, and Jack knew that nothing could be achieved before Monday.

He was about to return to his office when, on impulse, he turned towards the bank. For some reason he had an urge to see Thuli Nyembe in her work environment.

He could not believe he had been going into the same bank at least two or three times a month for most of his adult life and had never seen her there before. He guessed that she worked behind the counters or perhaps as a secretary, and wondered how long she had worked there. Maybe he had seen her and never really noticed her. That seemed unlikely; not to notice a woman as beautiful as she was.

He walked around the bank trying to spot Thuli. He looked behind the counters and into the back offices that were visible through the glass wall separating them from the counters.

He must have looked suspicious because a security guard walked over, surreptitiously releasing the catch on his holster as he approached.

Jack immediately put his hands up in front of him and identified himself. Under the suspicious guard's watchful eye, he removed and showed his badge, and the guard reluctantly accepted that Jack was not a potential bank robber.

Jack then realised that he would have to give a reason for being there, and mentioned Thuli's name. He felt as gauche as a teenager, like a raw schoolboy caught sneaking a peep through the window of the girls' changing room.

The guard pointed wordlessly at a discreet sign on one of the office doors – 'Thuli Nyembe, Commercial Manager'.

Commercial Manager! Oh boy, he really was out of his league. Damn, why did he always end up fancying women who were never likely to give him a second glance? He was about to walk away when he heard her voice behind him.

"Hello, Detective. Do you have any news for me?"

Jack whipped round and smiled sheepishly.

"Well, actually, I just wanted to hear how you were doing, staying at your grandmother's house."

"It's no hardship staying with Gogo. She is fantastic and has always been there for me. She seems to be unlike herself at the moment, though – very absent-minded and distracted."

"She is getting quite old, you know," said Jack sympathetically.

"Perhaps," answered Thuli sharply, "but a person doesn't just go senile overnight. She has always been as sharp as a button. I hope she is not getting sick or something."

Rebuffed, Jack turned to leave. "Please give her my respects."

"Why don't you give them to her yourself," suggested Thuli with a disarming smile. "I'm just heading home and was about to catch a taxi because my car is in for a service. You could give me a lift, if you like."

Jack glowed with joy.

"Your chariot awaits you, then," he smiled happily, leading the way to his beloved silver Mazda 3 and carefully opening the door for her.

Thuli looked quickly around the car, impressed to see that it was spotless both inside and out, with no dangly mascots or gaudy seat covers. She had always thought that the inside of a man's car said more about him than the outside. The outside of the car was what he projected to the world; the inside was who he really was. She absolutely hated getting into a car with dirty seats, rubbish on the floor and blaring music. It was an instant turn-off, and several otherwise charming men had been left wondering what had happened when the magic faded as the car doors closed.

Thuli gave Jack a warm smile as he got into the car, which left him wondering what he had done to deserve such a glowing look.

It was a fifteen minute drive to Gogo's house in the location. The time was pleasantly filled with light conversation, broken by comfortable silences. Thuli found herself feeling as if she had known Jack for a long, long time.

Gogo was sitting on the stoep, crocheting one of the blankets she was constantly making for the children at the AIDS orphanage. She smiled when she saw Jack pull up in the driveway, a smile that widened when she saw Thuli climb out from the passenger seat. The situation is developing nicely, she thought contentedly.

Jack greeted her respectfully. For someone so small she was a formidable woman, a real lady, and most importantly, Thuli's grandmother. He was fairly sure that she did not disapprove of the friendship that seemed to be developing between himself and Thuli. He was determined not to ruin her good impression.

93

She quickly bustled about, making tea and bringing out some of the cake that always seemed to be available in her house.

Soon they were sitting on the stoep watching the Friday evening crowd coming home from work. The shebeen up the road was pumping out some lively music. They watched a couple of teenage boys, looking very cool with baggy pants and peak caps at unlikely angles, practising their dance moves while a trio of pretty teenage girls giggled and whispered behind their hands a short distance away.

A passing woman with a child on her back and another two tumbling around her ankles called out cheerfully. Gogo returned the greeting. It was all part of the communal life of the location, and Gogo reigned as queen.

"How's your investigation coming along?" she asked.

"It's an awful case, Mma," Jack answered, shaking his head sadly, "probably one of the most disturbing of my career."

"Tell me about it, my child," Gogo said comfortably.

Lulled into a sense of familiarity, and against his better judgement, Jack started telling them about the bones found in the old laundry. The story was vivid in his mind, as if he had actually been there when the tragedy had unfolded.

"There were two women, one older and one younger. It was the younger one we found first, with thick wire twisted around her wrist, fastened to a chain and then to a metal bar that was probably once attached to the wall. She must have tried to free herself, breaking her wrist in the attempt. But her efforts were wasted and it's likely that she starved to death. Possibly she was bricked into the room alive, or maybe she died first and was then bricked in. Whatever the timing, she had a long and lonely death.

"The older woman was struck in the face by a large and powerful man. This broke her jaw. As she fell, she hit her head on a rock. She did not die immediately. Whether she was conscious or unconscious we cannot tell, but it took her a few hours to die."

He was staring at his hands as he told the story, trying to blot out the image of their deaths, recounting the story in a matter-of-fact way.

"But the worst part is the children ..."

"Children? I thought there was only one child." Gogo sounded faint and breathless.

"No," Jack replied, his eyes on the scenes of township life. "There were seven children, aged between about six and eleven. They were beaten before they died. There was not one who did not have broken bones, even the tiniest of them."

Jack heard a choking noise and looked up to see Gogo gasping and clutching her chest. He was just in time to catch her as she toppled off her chair and sank to the ground.

Desperately shouting to Thuli to call the ambulance, he administered CPR, hoping that the training he had received last year would pay off.

He cursed himself for his careless talk that had obviously affected the old lady so badly. It was his own fault for speaking so freely. He had felt so comfortable and familiar in their presence, as if he was with his own family, and that had loosened his tongue. He prayed that his thoughtlessness had not killed her.

The ambulance seemed to take forever to arrive, but at last Gogo was on her way to the hospital. Jack and Thuli followed in his car, Thuli tense and silent. Her horror at the story was nothing compared to her horror and fear that her grandmother might die.

"I'm so sorry," said Jack humbly. "I didn't know she had a weak heart. I should be more careful about what I say in front of people."

"But my grandmother doesn't have a weak heart," answered Thuli dully. "She saw the doctor just three weeks ago for a check-up and he said she had the heart of an eighteen-year-old. Oh God, please don't let her die!"

She started to sob, so Jack stopped the car on the side of the road and took her gently in his arms. He waited until she had regained control of herself, then he took out his fresh handkerchief and dried her tears.

"Are you feeling a little stronger?" he asked. Thuli nodded. "Then let's get to the hospital to hear what the doctor has to say."

It was about two hours before the doctor came out to where Jack and Thuli were sitting. Thuli was immediately reassured to see him smile comfortingly as he approached.

"Well, you'll be pleased to know that your grandmother did not have a heart attack after all," he said with a smile. "However, she seems to have suffered from a panic attack."

"A panic attack?" echoed Thuli. "Could a sad story bring on a panic attack?"

"Who knows?" answered the doctor. "Sometimes it's the unlikeliest thing that causes an attack.

"You should go through and talk to your grandmother," he said. "She said she wanted to talk to you. Both of you, she said."

Thuli and Jack thanked him and quietly entered the door that the doctor had indicated to them.

Gogo was sitting up in bed looking old and frail. Thuli's heart twisted with the thought that it was only a matter of time before the old lady would be gone.

She went up and took her grandmother's hand.

"You gave us such a big fright, Gogo," she said gently. "We thought you were having a heart attack." A tear slid down her cheek and she brushed it away before her grandmother could see it.

"I am so sorry, Mma," said Jack humbly. "I believe it was the story I was telling you that upset you so badly. I'll not bring my cases into your home again, I promise."

Gogo shook her head and put out her other hand to reach for Jack's. He held her frail hand in his, feeling a surge of affection for the indomitable old lady. His own grandmother had died when he was just ten, but his memories were of a martinet with a sjambok and a fierce temper. Not anything like the gentle and loving Mma Nyembe.

"Jack, come and sit here with me for a moment. Thuli, I'm thirsty. Please get me some water."

Thuli knew she was being dismissed. Although she was itching to know why, she went with good grace, waiting at least ten minutes before returning with a bottle of still water from the Magaliesberg Mountains.

When she returned, Gogo looked more peaceful. But Jack looked as if he had been struck by lightning.

He suggested to Thuli that Gogo needed her rest, and offered to take her home. At first Thuli refused, but Gogo insisted, and soon Jack and Thuli were on their way back to the location.

The silence was not the comfortable silence of before. It was obvious that Jack was dealing with whatever Gogo had told him. He was not in a talkative mood. Thuli did not want to ask outright what Gogo had said, and Jack was not telling. Even her gentle probing did not bring forth any satisfactory answers.

They sat in silence as they drove the few kilometres to the location. In the lights of the oncoming cars, Thuli tried to decipher the expression on Jack's face. She eventually came to the conclusion that it was disbelief; horrified disbelief. What could Gogo possibly have said to him to cause such an expression?

Chapter 28

As Jack walked into the station on Monday morning, stopping at the coffee machine on his way to his desk, Joe called him over.

"I have found Josephine Vilikazi's daughter," he said. "She's living in Johannesburg and is willing to come in tomorrow to speak to us. She said she remembers her mother's disappearance well, and has some odds and ends that her father put together when he was trying to find her."

"Good, get her to come in. Also, I'd like you to trace who owned all the farms between here and Bethel in 1964."

"You sound as if you have some new information. What makes you sure 1964 is the relevant year?" asked Joe.

"I have a witness who might have seen the abduction and deaths of the women and children," he said in a matter-of-fact voice.

Joe gaped at him in disbelief. "Yo! How'd you do that? Any witness would have to be in their seventies."

"You wouldn't believe me if I told you. The coincidence is almost too unbelievable."

He leaned forward and said quietly, "I want you to keep this to yourself for the moment. I've the strangest feeling about this crime. Even though it happened so many years ago, it still feels fresh and dangerous somehow. My witness is Thuli Nyembe's grandmother. Do you remember Thuli?"

"Who could forget her? She must be the prettiest woman in this town by a mile. When will we see the grandmother?"

"She's in hospital at the moment. It's a long story. I'll bring her in this afternoon to make a formal statement if she's strong enough."

Jack went to his desk and sat down. He leaned back, put his feet up, and stared at the ceiling. He needed time to think. Not that he had thought about anything else all weekend. The old lady's revelations had been the only thing on his mind the entire time.

He had hoped to spend some time over the weekend with Thuli but was worried that he would break his promise to the old woman and let something slip. His mates on the football team had mocked him about his game, and he ended up having to buy a couple of rounds of drinks before he was able to live down their suggestions that his love life was affecting his football.

Love was perhaps a strong word for what he felt, but he was definitely interested. You would have to be deaf, dumb and blind not to be. At the

97

moment, though, Thuli was proving to be a distraction from his primary concern; a wonderful distraction, but a problem nevertheless.

It frustrated him terribly that the person who seemed to fit the crime in every way appeared to be in the clear. Van Tonder was the senior officer in charge of the investigation into Josephine Vilikazi's disappearance. Apart from that, he had owned the house where the bodies were found.

Unfortunately, he had not lived there at the relevant time. Jack leaned over and picked up the file that Harry at the council had copied for him. He checked it again. There was no mistake. Van Tonder had bought the house in 1974, ten years after what he had started to call the massacre.

From the way the bones had been found, it was unlikely that the bodies had been moved years after the event. Those bodies had been placed there at the time, so whoever lived in the house in 1964 was likely to be the killer, not someone who moved in ten years later.

A sudden thought struck Jack. The title deed should also show the seller. He opened the file again and read through the document. The seller was listed as Jacobus Johannes Mostert. That was who he needed to find! That was the man living in the house at the critical time, and probably the murderer.

Half an hour later he was back where he started. A quick check showed that Jacobus Johannes Mostert had died in December 1973 at the age of fifty-one. If Mostert was the murderer, he had managed to escape retribution, at least in this world. Jack slammed the file down on his desk in anger and frustration.

Everyone he might want to speak to was either dead or senile. Not that Van Tonder was senile. He tried to give that impression, but Jack had seen a shrewd brain behind those veiled eyes.

Chapter 29

Doctor Sheila Henderson looked every inch the pathologist when Jack entered the examination theatre at the mortuary. Handel's Hallelujah Chorus was blaring out of an iPhone docking station on the table. Jack was more into jazz, not this sort of orchestral/choral music, but the music was familiar to him. Sheila was peering through a magnifying glass at some delicate bone fragments, and making meticulous notes in her file.

She looked up at Jack as he came in, giving him a smile that transformed her into a lovely young woman.

"Jack! Just the man I was looking for."

"You have news for me?" he asked.

"News? In a manner of speaking, I suppose it is," she said enigmatically.

Jack perched on the high metal chair next to the operating table and waited while Sheila gathered some notes together.

"Do you have a cause of death for me?"

"I thought it was time of death you were interested in," she said, "but we could do cause of death first if you wish."

"No, time of death first, if you please," he requested.

"It seems pretty certain that the deaths occurred approximately forty-five years ago, so about 1965, give or take one or two years either way. I'm afraid I can't be more definite than that. Apparently there was a twin-tub washing machine in that laundry, and I have it on excellent authority that the first twin-tubs were introduced into South Africa in the late 1950s."

"That ties in with other evidence I have gathered."

"You have evidence of a specific date?" she asked eagerly.

"I do. But first, please, can you give me the cause of death of the children?" he asked politely but firmly.

"Well, there I've hit a problem. I've examined the injuries the children sustained, and though they might all have been in shock and definitely in pain, the injuries would not have been sufficient to kill them. There is no evidence of gunshots or stabbing. Whatever they died of is not evident in the remains."

"So, could it have been something like poison?"

"Unlikely. I have ruled out some poisons, although there are many poisons which would not have left traces in the bones. As I said, cause of death cannot be identified by the bones."

"So, what could have killed them?" asked Jack. "Any wild hypotheses will do at this stage."

"Well, they could have been smothered, or drowned," Sheila said, trying to come up with some theories. "To be honest, this has completely stumped me. And I don't like being stumped."

"That makes two of us," Jack said morosely.

"So, what is this evidence you have found that establishes the date?"

"A teacher and her pupils disappeared in December 1964. They were never seen again. These bones could be the remains of those people."

"The timing seems right, but what about the second woman?"

"She was the younger sister of the older woman. Apparently, she was severely mentally challenged. Her mental age was around six."

"That poor, poor woman," said Sheila sadly. "She must have gone through hell, her sister dead, and being subjected to the most horrific abuse. I can only guess what she must have gone through."

"Whoever did this must be some kind of sociopath," said Jack grimly. "I just pray that he is still alive after all this time and will be brought to justice, to face some of the reality of the people whose lives he took, and the families they left behind."

"Amen to that!" said Sheila.

Chapter 30

Jack tried to schedule his appointment with Mma Nyembe for a time when he knew Thuli would be at work. He wanted to protect Thuli from the revelations that he felt sure were likely to emerge from the interview. But Thuli was a force to be reckoned with. She was determined to be at her grandmother's side, and had taken the afternoon off from the bank. Both Jack and Gogo tried to change her mind, but Thuli was having none of it. She was sure that her grandmother's panic attack was linked to the case in some way, and refused to leave her.

Jack was more successful when he insisted that Thuli would not be sitting in on the interview with her grandmother. He left her sitting in the waiting area, angrily leafing through a Panorama magazine, as he led her grandmother through to the interview room.

Joe was seated in his usual corner, ready to take notes and control the video camera.

"First, for the record Mma, what is your name?"

"Anna, Anna Nyembe."

"And how old are you?"

"At the beginning of the winter, I'll be sixty-one years old."

"And where do you live?"

"In the location, here in Standerton."

"Your address, Mma."

"129 Geelhout Street."

"That's good. Now we can begin."

It was over an hour later when Jack led Anna Nyembe back into the waiting area. Thuli jumped up to greet her grandmother, shocked by the transformation that had taken place. Gogo looked every bit as old as her years, and more.

"What have you been doing to her?" she demanded angrily.

"Shush, child," said Gogo calmingly. "Detective Malepo has helped me to share a terrible burden that I've carried with me all my life. I feel more at peace now. One day soon, when the time is right, I will tell you the whole story, but in the meantime we'll leave Detective Malepo in peace so that he can find the man who did these terrible things."

Jack watched Thuli lead her grandmother to their car. He then returned to the interview room to watch the recording. He needed to try to recreate in his mind the very different world that his father and grandfather had grown up in. Those were times when the lives of black people were considered cheap; when the disappearance of a group of nine people, seven of them small children, would not even have been investigated.

Mma Nyembe had agreed to return the following day, to tell the rest of her story and to bring it up to date. Jack was so gripped with this case. It was almost an obsession for him to find the killer and bring him to justice.

Chapter 31

Josephine Vilikazi's daughter was a teacher, like her mother before her. Tall and elegant, she looked younger than her fifty-nine years.

Joe met her at the front desk and brought her into one of the small interview rooms that ran along the edge of the open-plan office where the detectives spent their working hours. She declined his offer of tea, holding firmly onto the old Bakers biscuit tin that he tried to relieve her of as she sat down.

A few minutes later Jack entered, introducing himself as the detective in charge of the investigation. Joe seated himself inconspicuously in the corner to control the video camera that would record the interview.

"Thank you for coming in, Mma," said Jack respectfully.

"I have been waiting for this meeting all my life, Detective. I would have travelled halfway across the world to get the chance to find out what happened to my mother."

"What has my colleague told you about our investigation?"

"Just that it was possible that he had some information which might relate to my mother's disappearance."

"There are just a few formalities we need to go through before we start, Mma. First, for the record, what is your name?"

"Agnes Vilikazi."

"And how old are you?"

"I am fifty-five years old."

"And where do you live?"

"In Germiston. 22 Burton Street, Germiston."

"Tell me, Mma, how old were you when your mother disappeared?" asked Jack.

"I was just ten years old."

"Do you remember much of what happened?"

"Some of it I remember; some I had from my father and my elder sister. He was a changed man after my mother and her sister disappeared. He spent the next five years trying to find them."

"What made him stop?"

"He didn't. One day, he didn't come home. They found him lying in an alley in town with half his head blown away. He'd been shot at close range."

"Did they find out who killed him?"

"That was the sixties, Detective," she said bitterly. "Who cared how a black man came to be shot? There was an investigation of sorts, but nothing came of it."

He looked meaningfully at Joe, who made a note in his notebook: Follow up on the death of Hector Vilikazi.

Jack indicated the tin that Agnes was holding on her lap.

"You have something in the tin you would like to show us?" he asked.

She nodded grimly, and carefully prized open the lid. She laid it reverently on the table in front of her and lifted out a hardcover notebook, which she handed to Jack.

"It is a bit difficult to decipher anything. My father did not have the advantage of an education so his spelling is phonetic, but it is generally possible to make sense of it. This is a record of his investigations, for what they were worth. It records the people he spoke to and the evidence he tried to piece together. I have read it over and over again. The fact is, he actually found out nothing."

Jack took a few moments to page through the book. She was right about it being difficult to read.

"Can I keep this? I promise to return it when our investigation is over."

Agnes reached over as if to snatch it back, but then reluctantly withdrew her hand, nodding. This was her best chance of getting answers to her parents' deaths.

"We'd like to know a little more about your mother," said Jack. "Where did she teach?"

"It was a tiny farm school halfway between Bethel and Standerton, mainly for children too young to walk into Standerton or Bethel every day."

"And you spoke of your mother's sister. Did she also work at the school?"

"No. She was at the school every day because my mother was taking care of her. But she was not able to work. Elsie was born about twenty years after my mother. She grew to be a woman physically, but mentally she was like a small child all her life. When my grandmother died, my mother took over the care of her sister. She was more like a younger sister to us than an aunt, though to look at her, you would have taken her for a woman just like any other."

Jack nodded. The black community tended to look after its own. Children born with particular challenges are cared for by the family, with very few individuals finding their way into institutions or hospitals.

"What about the pupils?" he asked. "Did you know them?"

"The pupils were the children of the farm workers. I doubt there were ever more than twelve pupils. My sister, Evaline, and I went there when we were little. We attended until I was eight years old and Evaline was twelve.

"When my mother disappeared, we were both at a school in Standerton. Evaline was considered old enough by then to take care of me. And she did so, as well as any mother."

Agnes smiled for the first time.

"You and your sister had a good relationship, then?" asked Jack.

"She was wonderful. After my father died, she was convinced that we were in danger. So she took me to live with my grandmother in Germiston while she went to work as a maid for an English family in the town. They were very good to her and she stayed with them for over thirty years, until they died, first the old man and then the old lady."

"She was happy, then?" asked Jack.

"I suppose we were both happy, although neither of us could forget what had happened to our parents. She kept this tin all the years. Then she became ill with tuberculosis. I was with her when she was dying. She gave the tin to me and told me never to stop trying to find out what happened."

"Going back to when your mother disappeared. Were you aware of any other people who had disappeared?" Jack asked.

"Well, there was my mother's sister, Elsie. And of course there were the children. There were seven children with my mother when she went missing. That was what my father kept telling the police, but that fat policeman insisted that my mother had run away because my father was beating her."

"Was he beating her?" he asked.

"Never!" Agnes said indignantly. "Our father never raised a hand to our mother or to us, all our lives. He was a quiet and gentle man who worked on the farm as a dairyman. I never heard him raise his voice, not once."

"And the parents of these children," Jack probed further, "did they not try to follow up what had happened to their children?"

"Of course! A mother doesn't just sit back when her child disappears, and one woman lost two children that day. The whole village turned out to look for my mother and the children. The farmer, Mr Serfontein, offered a reward to anyone who could help to find them. But we never found anything. They visited the hospital, the morgue, the police station... no one had seen them. It was like that story of the Pied Piper; as if they had disappeared into the mountain."

"Did the police investigate?"

"The police!" she snapped contemptuously. "They were absolutely useless. For all the notice they took, it might have been some chickens that had gone missing."

"When did this all happen?"

"It was just before Christmas, in 1964. My sister and I had saved for ages and had bought our mother a scarf for Christmas. We never got the chance to give it to her."

Jack looked at the tin Agnes was holding firmly on her lap.

"Do you mind if I take a look?"

Agnes reluctantly handed it over.

Jack drew out a faded and brittle sheet of paper, obviously torn out of a school exercise book. It had a wax crayon drawing of a field with huge brightly coloured flowers and what appeared to be cows hovering in the sky. In the bottom corner, in a neat handwriting, were the words, 'Very good, Aletta'. The date was 3 December 1964.

Jack wondered if Aletta was one of the little heaps of bones lying in the mortuary.

A browning envelope at the bottom of the tin held a faded blue scarf with a white mathematical design along its edges. None of the other items shed any light on the case, other than the names on the little pile of drawings, which Jack made a note of before placing all the drawings and mementos back into the tin.

He felt a tear prick his eye and gave himself a little shake. He could not afford to be sentimental about this case.

"Mma, I wonder if we could take a DNA sample from you? You've probably realised that we have found some remains that we believe may have been your mother. We're hoping to isolate DNA which might either prove or disprove our theory."

"What do you need? I'll do anything. Whichever way she met her end, it'd be good to be able to lay her in the grave next to my father, and it would give me peace to know I have kept my promise to my sister."

"It's nothing very difficult. Just a swab from your mouth will be sufficient."

He thanked her and left Joe to deal with the formalities of obtaining the DNA sample.

Chapter 32

Jack was frustrated and irritable. He hated being cooped up in the office. But this case did not have any current physical evidence, and most of the investigation involved research into files that were archived decades ago.

The few items found in the bricked-in laundry were dead ends. There was nothing there which could shed light on the case, and they had already managed to pinpoint the time of the murders. But it was more difficult patching together the rest of the tale.

He had spent the previous four hours putting all the details that they had discovered about the case onto the chalkboard in his office, hoping to get some sort of clue as to the identity of the killer. Then he stood staring at his notes for a further thirty minutes, hoping for a revelation.

He was finally distracted by Joe, who came into the office waving a sheet of paper at him.

"I have a list of farms between here and Bethel during the sixties. There are seven farms now, as three of them have since been subdivided, but in those days there were only four. The farm Morelig was owned by the Serfontein family, Jakkalsvlei by the Mostert family, Ventersrus by – you guessed it – the Venter family, and Klipfontein by the Stander family.

"Nothing owned by the Van Tonders, then?" asked Jack without much hope.

"Nope," said Joe, shaking his head.

Jack added the names to the board, hoping to see some sort of link.

"Another bloody blank wall!" he groaned, staring at the board. "I have so much information about the people and the events yet seem to be getting no further in finding the bloody culprit at all."

"You are getting too personally involved," suggested Joe.

"Just what are you implying?" demanded Jack defensively.

"Nothing, Jack. Yo, calm down, brother! I was just saying that you are getting too emotionally involved with the victims."

"Oh, I thought ..."

"What?" demanded Joe, clearly upset.

"I thought you were implying that I was getting too involved with Thuli Nyembe," mumbled Jack.

"Are you?" asked Joe.

"I wish I was. She is way out of my league," he said morosely. "I always seem to fancy women who would not look twice at me."

"Don't be so negative, I think she likes you. If you'd just take a chance and ask her out, she might just put you out of your misery ... and do us all a favour."

"Not while she is involved in a case I'm working on. You know how strict the boss is about mixing business with pleasure. I'd be suspended from the case in a minute."

"Then I suggest you solve this case quickly. You're very irritable at the moment, and you're taking it out on me."

"Never! I wouldn't dare," laughed Jack apologetically. Joe gave him a brotherly punch on the shoulder and harmony was restored.

He shut down his computer and cleared his desk. He needed to spend a few quiet hours thinking things through and trying to make sense of the information they had gathered.

Refusing Joe's suggestion of a drink at the football club, he picked up his jacket and was about to head home, when he stopped. Something that Joe had said was niggling at his subconscious and he turned again to stare at his board.

"What was that you said about the farms?" he asked again, trying to recapture his errant thoughts.

"There were four farms, Morelig, Jakkalsvlei, Ventersrus and Klipfontein."

"No, no, the owners of the farms."

"The Serfonteins, the Mosterts, the Venters and the Standers."

Jack pointed triumphantly at the name on his board.

"Mostert!" he shouted triumphantly. "The house was originally owned by a guy called Mostert. Where the hell is that title deed?"

He rummaged through his desk, scattering papers, not finding what he was looking for. Then he went through to a filing cabinet, returning with the title deed.

"Jacobus Johannes Mostert!" he shouted. "The owner of the property before Van Tonder was Jacobus Johannes Mostert."

"And?" asked Joe in bewilderment.

"Check the owners of the farms. One was owned by the Mostert family. Do you have the full name of the owner of that farm at the time?"

Joe went through his notes. He had not made a note of the full names of the owners. That meant another run-in with Harry at the council. It also meant that they would have to wait until the next day to get the answer. Jack's frustration was boiling over, so Joe decided that a tactical retreat was in order. He picked up his jacket and headed quickly out of the door before his partner could demand that he track down the colourful Harry at his home.

Chapter 33

Mma Anna Nyembe returned the following day, as promised. Rather than taking her into the interview, Jack suggested that they take a drive. He had printed out a map of the route to Jakkalsvlei as it appeared on the current maps.

"Where are we going?" she asked.

"You'll need to wait and see," he answered mysteriously.

Without Thuli hovering in the background, the old lady seemed calmer and Jack took his time to draw her story out.

"Now, Mma," Jack said quietly, "I want you to tell us the story of your life, in your own words. Tell me everything, no matter how trivial or irrelevant it may seem to you. Even things that might seem unimportant might have a bearing on the case; might lead us to the person who killed these women and children."

Mma Nyembe had spent the night thinking about the events and had already prepared herself for the task. She started haltingly, but soon lost herself in the story; the people and events that had shaped her life.

"I was born near the end of the Second World War. Not that we knew much about the war, or anything beyond our own little world in those days. Life on the farm was hard. My father left us when my younger sister was born. We were three girl children, no boys. My mother had no husband or brother to speak for us, so we could not get husbands. When she was sixteen, my older sister, Nandi, left to be the third wife of a man in the next village. But the man's first wife was very cruel to her, and she came back after three years, the same time that I did after witnessing the terrible crime I told you about yesterday. As I've already explained, I was pregnant. So was Nandi.

"Our babies were born in the winter of 1965. My baby, Patience, was a few weeks older than Nandi's son, Jacob.

"For the first few months after I arrived home, I was afraid that the policeman would come and find me. But soon I forgot about him, except in my dreams. The dreams came every night. I could hear the sound of the children laughing as they splashed in the water. I could feel the heat of the rocks next to the vlei that steamed when the cold water splashed on them. I could hear the sound that Mma Josie's head made when it hit the rock."

She stopped for a while, memories crowding around her, then she continued.

"We had a small piece of land in the village where we kept four goats for milk. When I was working in Standerton, I had helped one of the women who made cheese out of leftover milk. So, one day when we had too much milk from our goats, I decided to try to make that cheese again. It took me a few weeks and quite a lot of wasted milk, but at last I managed to make the cheese. It was very good, and my mother and sisters liked it very much. I thought it would be a good idea to make that cheese and sell it on the side of the road, near the kuka shop. My small enterprise started slowly, but soon more and more people were buying my cheese.

"After about a year, I had made enough money to buy another goat. I could then make more cheese. The people liked my cheese very much and often white people came from the town to buy it. Soon I bought another goat, and then another, until I had twelve goats. I taught my younger sister, Tembeni, to make the cheese. We sold everything we made.

"One day, I decided to take some of my cheese to the supermarket in the town to see if the manager would buy some to sell there. He was a good man. He said he would sell it if I could make sure that it was packed in special paper, that it always weighed exactly the same amount each time, and that there was at least forty kilograms of the cheese delivered every month.

"That was a lot of cheese, more than I had ever made before. When I did my sums, I knew that I would need to have at least twenty goats. I would need a special building to milk the goats in, with a cold room to store the fresh milk and the cheese once it was made, and another special room where I could prepare the cheese. I'd also need a way of getting the cheese to the supermarket every month.

"I knew I couldn't afford to build a special building, so I found one belonging to the local chief. It was a shebeen before and had a big walk-in fridge. The owner of the shebeen had been arrested by the police for running an illegal business. They beat him, and then they took all his money, all his beer and mampoer. He hanged himself from a big oak tree in the mealie field. I hoped that would not happen to me because I was starting to think that I could make this cheese factory work.

"My mother and Nandi thought I was mad. They didn't want to help me with the cheese. Nandi complained that I was not looking after Patience. She said that I was leaving her to take care of the little ones while I was playing at being an important businesswoman.

"It was true. I could not love Patience. Every time I looked at her I remembered the bad smell of my uncle and his hand across my mouth to stop me screaming. I did not want the baby anywhere near me. Patience and Jacob played together and Nandi looked after them, while I spent more and more time working in my little factory.

"Setting it up was very expensive. I used all the money I had saved and still needed more. Then I had an idea about who I could get more money from.

"I walked twenty kilometres into Standerton, to the house of my uncle and his wife, the uncle who was the father of Patience. I told him that I had a girl child and that he was the father. I said that if he did not give me two hundred rand, I would tell his wife and the chief that he had made me pregnant. His wife would leave him and the chief would order him to pay my mother three goats. He would be shamed in front of all the people of the location.

"He was very angry and hit me across my face. My lip bled from the deep cut. But this time I was older and was no longer afraid of him. In fact, I was pleased that he had hit me. I told him that now I would tell everyone he had beaten me again, as he had done when he made me pregnant. I would show them my face, all cut and bruised.

"The next day, I went back to his house. He gave me one hundred and fifty-two rand. He said it was all the money he had. It was enough for me to pay for all the things I needed for my factory, so I started off for home."

She stopped again to collect her thoughts.

"I started to walk home. I was just leaving the location when I saw a Black Maria coming down the road. I ran quickly to the bushes to hide because I did not have a pass to be in Standerton. The two policemen did not see me, but I saw them. One of them was that fat policeman, the one who hit Mma Josie and took the children.

"They drove past me without stopping. When they had gone, I found my underclothes were soaked through. I had wet myself from fear and had to change my underwear before I could go on."

Jack stopped to check the map – the road seemed to head off in the wrong direction, and he had to check the directions. Gogo remained silent until he started the car again.

"My younger sister, Tembeni is a clever girl. She went to school until she was sixteen years old. She was such a help. She found out that I'd need a certificate from the health department to sell my cheese to a supermarket.

"We worked hard for almost four months to make that factory ready for the inspectors to come. We scrubbed the goats, the buckets, the cloths, the sieves. We hosed down the floors until that workshop was spotless. It had clean white tiles and shiny metal tables. The inspectors spent two hours going through the factory. They took samples of the milk and the cheese, and then they left.

"Tembeni and I were so worried, and I couldn't sleep. The dreams were worse than ever. We had spent almost all of my savings, and if we did not get the licence we would lose it all. But we worried for nothing. A week later, the inspector came back with a certificate signed by the magistrate, with a big red stamp in one corner. I went to that supermarket and bought a frame, and we hung the certificate on the wall in the workshop. I have it still, hanging now in my house.

"I invited the manager of the supermarket to visit our little factory. He was very pleased, and we signed a contract for fifty kilograms of cheese every month, in weekly deliveries. A few weeks later, we delivered our first order. Two weeks after that, the money was in my bank. We had begun our business, which we called Imbuzi Esasayo. It means happy goat.

"Soon, I was very busy. I was buying milk from other farmers and had four women working for me, making the cheese. We started delivering to other supermarkets, and after some years we made enough money to build a fine new house for my mother, my sisters, our children and me, in the location here in Standerton, with a field next door for the goats. I also started to put money away for Patience's education and her wedding.

"As the years passed by, I had started feeling differently about Patience. Yet she was already almost a teenager and was happier being with Nandi and Jacob. I felt hurt, although it was my own fault that my child didn't want to be with me because I had rejected her when she was young. I tried to make up for my neglect by buying her presents and pretty clothes. She liked the presents, but that did not change how she felt about me.

"Things were going well for our family. We had a nice house in the location and money in the bank. We even had enough money to buy a small van. I was too scared to drive it, but Tembeni quickly learned how. Our mother was getting old and forgetful, and in my thirtieth year, Nandi took over the running of the house. It was a peaceful and happy life.

"Then, when Patience was about fourteen years old, Nandi found out that she was sleeping with one of the local tsotsis. She went out to look for her and found her in a bad part of town in a shebeen, drinking and smoking dagga. Nandi brought her home, beat her with a sjambok, and locked her into her room. Patience went mad in that room, screaming and kicking the door. The next day when she was in the bathroom she managed to climb through the small window of the toilet and ran away.

"All the people of the location helped us to search, but we could not find her. Nandi and I went to every place we could think of to try and find out where she had gone. We even went to Johannesburg, thinking that the city life would have called her. But that place is so big that we could not find her. We came home without our child.

"Nandi cried. She had always wanted Patience and Jacob to marry, and now her dreams were useless. At first she was sad, and then she became angry.

She said that even if Patience came back she would tell her to go away, that we didn't need her there.

"But she did not get the chance to tell Patience that. It was three years before we saw her again. She was very pregnant, and she was dying. I remember that morning like it was yesterday. Every morning when I awoke, I would go out to let the goats into the field to graze. That morning, as I walked towards the gate, I saw a small figure lying on the pathway. It was Patience. She could not breathe properly and was very thin, with sores all over her face and body.

"I called Nandi, and together we carried her to her old room, where we laid her on her old bed. Her skin was an ugly grey colour and covered with scabs, and her eyes were unfocused. We could not understand how she had managed to find her way back to us. She must have had an angel watching over her.

"The doctor came. He shook his head and told us he had seen this illness before. He told us she would die soon, and probably the baby too. He said that sometimes the babies survived, but in this case it would be a miracle.

"Nandi and I took turns nursing Patience. She recovered enough to recognise us and tell us a little of her story ... that part that she was prepared to share with us.

"She had been in Johannesburg as we suspected, living with that tsotsi. He found customers for her and then he took the money she earned working as a prostitute on the streets of the city.

"She was happy with that life for a few years, until she got ill. She lived in a flat in Hillbrow and had pretty clothes to wear. One day, she got a bad cold that did not go away. She felt too ill to work, but that tsotsi forced her to go out every day and every night.

"The sickness got worse. She got thin and the men did not want to sleep with her any more. He said she was worthless and a waste of money and threw her out of the flat, keeping all her clothes and money. She had nothing, and the only way she knew how to make money was to sleep with men and get paid for it. She tried to work on the streets without the tsotsi, but that was very dangerous. One night, two men attacked her. They said she was trying to kill them with her sickness.

"She was lying in an alleyway with her face badly cut and bloody and her ribs broken, when a holy sister from the church found her and took her to the hospital. On the second morning, the sister came and told her that she was very lucky, and that the baby had survived the attack. Until that moment, Patience did not even know that she was pregnant. How the baby survived her mother's beating is a miracle.

"After she got out of the hospital she went back to that tsotsi to tell him about the child, but he swore at her and told her to go away. He said that if she did not leave he would call the police. He did not want any children, and he did not want a sick and pregnant girlfriend.

"She was frightened and alone, so Patience did what I did twenty years earlier in a similar situation – she returned to her home and her family. But it was too late. The disease had eaten away her body, and only the little life growing inside her had the will to live.

"The doctor warned us that Patience was not likely to survive childbirth. And he was right, the arrival of the child was the end of Patience's life. But that baby was not ready to die. We named her Thuli, as Patience had asked us to do. We buried Patience in the churchyard, near the willow tree where she and Jacob had played so happily together as children.

"I didn't want to make the same mistakes with Thuli that I had made with Patience. From that first day, when I saw the little honey coloured child with her soft brown hair, I loved her with all my heart, as if she was my own child. It was a love I could never give to Patience. My heart was very sad that I had missed that with my own child, and sad for Patience that I could not give her my love. I felt that her unhappy childhood and early end were a result of the terrible things that happened to me as a young woman. I was determined that that would not happen to Thuli.

"Thuli grew to be a happy little girl; bright and inquisitive. Every day, I would spend hours with her, playing and teaching her to talk. I watched her grow from a baby into a child. Too soon it was time for her to go to school.

"I decided not to send her to the school in the location, and she started at the Montessori school in the town. Nandi was angry with me, saying I was giving the child ideas above her place. But on the matter of her education, I was determined. Thuli was quick to learn and was soon top of her class.

"In the meantime Jacob completed his schooling and did very well. He wanted to go to the university, but Nandi did not want him to leave Standerton. She said she did not have the money to pay for his studies. Jacob and I were good friends, and he told me how badly he wanted to study further. Eventually, we thought up a good story. Jacob told his mother that he had been given a bursary, and persuaded her to allow him to go. In fact, I paid his fees, on condition that if he did not complete his studies, or failed any courses, he'd have to pay me back.

"He did not really need that threat because he was a good and serious student. He graduated from the university in Pretoria in just five years with an accounting degree. Nandi missed him very much and was angry with me for encouraging him to go. She couldn't understand why I wanted the children to have the best possible education. She felt that this turned them away from their culture, and that she would lose Jacob if he became a big-shot businessman.

"I think Jacob understood how sad and angry she was. He was patient and loving with her always, making sure he caught the taxi home very often, though I'm sure he would rather have stayed with his friends in Pretoria over the weekends.

"He was never one of the wild tsotsis. I think what happened to Patience made a deep and lasting impression on him.

"When Jacob turned twenty-one, I bought him a second-hand Volkswagen Beetle. He loved that car and came home more often. Nandi was jealous that I had bought him an expensive present. She said he would kill himself on the road home from Pretoria, and that I would be responsible for his death.

"It was around that time that I decided that the cheese factory was doing well enough and that I did not need to spend every day at the office. Tembeni was married to a pastor and had three small children. We decided to employ a manager. We were very lucky to find a young white man, Gerrit Gous, who took over the day-to-day running of the business.

Gerrit was full of good ideas. Every Monday, he would come to my kitchen. We would drink tea and talk about his plans, and about what was happening at the factory.

"Tembeni and I soon came to trust him completely. In fact, he is there to this day. It was one of the best decisions of our lives because the business has prospered. We now have a very wide range of products and employ nearly one hundred people.

"After completing his articles in a big Pretoria accounting practice, Jacob returned to Standerton and took over as Finance Manager of the business. I think he did it mostly for his mother, but it has made me very happy and proud that Jacob has joined the business.

"It was only two years after Jacob returned that Nandi died. I was worried that Jacob might decide to return to the city, but he seemed happy in Standerton. He soon got married and had children of his own.

"Jacob and Gerrit have become good friends. Their children attend the Montessori school together, the same school Thuli started at when she was a little girl.

"Eventually, the business changed from a partnership into a company, with the shares divided equally between myself, Tembeni, Thuli, Jacob and Gerrit with Gerrit as the CEO. It has prospered, and provided a lot of employment in the town.

"Thuli was not like many other clever children who think they are better than others who are not so clever. She was very good and patient with those who were slower to learn. That was how she came to make friends with Katie van Tonder. That Katie was always a ray of sunshine in our lives. She spent many afternoons in my kitchen, with Thuli helping her with her spelling and reading.

"It was a waste of time, in the end. When Katie was about twelve years old, her mother took her to a special doctor who said she was dyslexic. I had not heard that word before, but when Thuli told me what it was, it all made sense to me. Katie was never stupid. She just struggled with words. It was perhaps a strange friendship as far as others could see, but it was a strong friendship that has lasted to this day.

"We were pleased that Thuli and Katie were friends, although Katie usually came to our house, where she was always welcome. For some reason, Thuli did not like to go to Katie's house, even though her mother, Julie, was always kind to her.

"When it was time for her to go to high school, I did not want Thuli to go to the local high school, which did not achieve very good results. I wanted her to get the best education money could buy, so I asked my customers in Johannesburg which was the best school. One of my oldest customers had two daughters at St Andrew's School for Girls. He had known Thuli since she was a child, and recommended her to the principal.

"Even though we had that recommendation, there were very strict standards, so Thuli had to take an entrance test. I was so proud the day she walked into that school, looking so beautiful in her school uniform! It cost a lot of money, but I wanted her to have all the advantages I never had as a child. In my heart, I hoped it would make up for how I had treated Patience.

"Thuli made me very proud there, with her studies and with her sports. She had many friends, and was a prefect in her final year. But Katie was still the friend she loved best. During the school holidays, they spent every moment together.

"When Thuli finished school she had no problems getting into the university in Johannesburg to do her Bachelor degree and then her MBA. When she finished studying, I thought she would go and work in some big company in Johannesburg, or maybe even in America. But she chose to come back here, to her Gogo. Aish! It was one of the happiest days of my life when she became a manager at the bank. She has made us all so proud.

"When I think of our life now, it seems very far away from what people like me had before. Then, every day was a struggle just to survive. We had no chance of making our lives better. But now we have our home and a company that has given us security. Our children have a good education and a real chance to make something of themselves in this world. The good Lord has blessed us.

"I thought that our life was perfect and that I'd die knowing that Thuli was safe and secure. Now, I'm not so sure.

"Forty-five years! It is about forty-five years since I turned and ran away from that vlei.

"The last time I really thought about Mma Josie and Mma Elsie and the children was about thirty years ago, when I was looking for money from my uncle. That was the day that I saw the two policemen in the Black Maria.

"It all faded from my memory, only returning in the occasional dream to disturb my sleep. Now, those people have risen from the dead. They are asking me why I kept silent all these years.

"I see their faces now as if it was yesterday that I turned and ran for my life. They will not let me go to my rest until we have punished the person who killed them.

"Now I know what it means to be haunted."

She had been talking as much to herself as to Jack. Having come to the end of her story she suddenly became aware that they had slowed down and looked around her.

"I have seen this place before," she said.

"Do you recognise it?" asked Jack

"Stop!" she said. Jack pulled up on a small koppie overlooking a modern farmhouse and outbuildings.

"What do you recognise?" he asked. "Is it the farmhouse?"

"No, that is new," she answered. She pointed.

"Look, the old farmhouse, and there, in the valley, do you see the vlei and those willow trees? That is the vlei where Mma Josephine and the children were attacked."

Chapter 34

Once they arrived back at the station and Mma Nyembe had headed home, Jack went over her story again. He now knew with certainty the location where the atrocity had happened, or at least begun, but it did not shed any light on the mystery surrounding who the murderer was.

He was making notes of significant points when Joe came in, clutching a sheet of paper.

"I've got that name."

"What name?" asked Jack absently, his mind on the screen.

"The owner of the farm, Jakkalsvlei."

Jack turned around, hope in his eyes.

"And the answer is...?" he prompted.

"Jacobus Andries Mostert. And before you ask, he died in 1966 at the age of seventy-eight."

"Did he have a son – maybe a policeman?"

"I don't know, but I think it is highly unlikely. The farm was inherited by his daughter, Nesta Serfontein, whose husband owned the adjacent farm - Morelig. It would have been very unusual for a girl to inherit in those days if she had had a male sibling."

"Is she still alive?"

"I don't know, but I'm going to find out."

Thuli had the sign outside her office turned to 'Closed'. She sat at her desk, gnawing at the cuticle on her left hand, a heavy frown on her face.

For the first time in her life, Thuli was finding her grandmother very frustrating. She obviously had critical information relating to the case and had told Jack Malepo all about it. But as much as Thuli tried, she was unable to extract anything from the usually talkative old woman. Days had passed since Gogo's visit to the station, and despite many attempts to find out the truth, Thuli was no wiser. Not only would her grandmother not talk to her about the case, but Jack also seemed to have evaporated into thin air.

Finally, she could bear it no longer. She picked up the phone and called Jack's number. When he answered, she launched into her excuse for the call without any polite preamble.

"You said you'd keep me informed about the case and let me know when I can move back into my house!" she said accusingly.

Jack's heart sank when he heard Thuli's voice. He had been trying to avoid speaking to her so that he would not be tempted to spill the beans. That story belonged to her grandmother, and it was up to her to tell Thuli.

"I'm sorry, but I'm afraid you will have to wait a little longer," he apologised. "I was hoping to clear up this case quite quickly, but it is proving more difficult than I thought. With luck, we'll have completed our work at your house before the end of the week. Obviously, we will carry out all the cleaning up and repair work on your house, and pay for any damage our investigation has caused."

"Great! That'll be useful because I have decided to break down that laundry completely and replace it with something entirely new and fresh. Fortunately, I don't believe in ghosts, and I don't fear any evil spirits."

"I'm impressed. That's surprisingly practical of you," he said admiringly.

"Why surprising? I've invested my life savings in the place and don't intend to lose it. I love that house and feel happy there. If it was haunted by the ghosts of those who were buried there, I wouldn't have that peaceful feeling that I have when I'm there."

Jack smiled to himself. Most of the women he had met would have been traumatised by the experience of finding human remains in their house. Thuli was definitely very different to most other women.

"I wanted to talk to you about my grandmother," said Thuli, hoping to get something out of him.

"How's she doing now?" Jack asked, bracing himself for the questions he did not want to answer. "Has she recovered from her fright?"

"Yes, that was what I wanted to talk to you about. She won't tell me what happened and I really need to know. Can you tell me?"

Jack smiled to himself. And here it comes, he thought.

"You know I can't answer that, Thuli. This is your grandmother's story. It's for her to tell you. I think she's waiting until the person responsible has been found. Give her some time."

Thuli was not satisfied, although she realised she was not going to get anything more out of Jack. Not being able to get sympathy from her grandmother, she called Julie and suggested getting together for coffee after work. Unfortunately, Julie was about to leave for the retirement home to visit her husband.

Julie listened sympathetically as Thuli complained bitterly about being kept in the dark about issues that were obviously important, and while she sympathised with Thuli, she gently refused to get involved.

Julie had been visiting Rick twice a week since he had gone to live at Woodlands. When she arrived at the retirement home, she was pleased to find that her husband seemed better than on her previous visit. He seemed genuinely interested, and listened intently as she recounted the events of the past few weeks. Julie described vividly the discovery of the bones and the progress of the investigation. She spoke of Thuli's frustration that her grandmother was not willing to tell her about what had happened, and that she seemed to be the main witness in the case.

Rick tried very hard to speak, and actually managed a few words. Julie picked up a few of these – like 'house', and 'Pa' – but was unable to make sense of what he was saying. Rick eventually gave up in frustration. His good hand clutched at the quilt, and Julie held it, feeling strangely protective. It was a new feeling for her. Rick had always been the head of the household, always in charge, expecting complete obedience although at the same time making sure that she was well cared for. Now things were different. She was the strong one; the person in control. She experienced a surge of love that she had not felt for many years.

She bent forward to kiss him as she left, and he watched her leave with sad and lonely eyes.

Chapter 35

There was an envelope on his desk when Jack returned to his office the next morning. The report inside confirmed that the DNA testing had shown Agnes Vilikazi to be the daughter of the older woman found in Thuli's house. That made the identification of the younger woman only a formality. Jack asked one of the junior officers to circulate the names of the children that he had copied from the wax crayon drawings in Agnes's biscuit tin. Perhaps the parents or relatives of those children were still around. Finding their children would provide them with answers that they had searched for at the time. It would give them an opportunity to finally bury their children.

Jack was also trying to decipher the diary of Hector Vilikazi's investigations, but it was a difficult and painstaking job. One word kept recurring – 'most' – which did not make sense.

Jack did not like to concede defeat, yet he felt that he had completely exhausted every avenue. He had picked up the telephone to call Thuli to tell her she could have her house back, when a small white-haired woman entered the office. She was followed by a triumphant looking Joe Bantu.

"Mrs Serfontein, please meet my colleague, Detective Malepo." Jack got to his feet automatically and greeted the little woman. For someone so small, she was very regal. Although he towered over her, Jack felt like a small boy in her presence. He looked enquiringly at Joe, unsure of the significance of her visit.

"Mrs Serfontein is the daughter of Jacobus Andries Mostert, who owned the farm Jakkalsvlei," Joe reminded Jack.

"Of course," exclaimed Jack, smiling his welcome. "It's very good of you to come to the station. I could have come to you."

"Nonsense!" snapped Nesta Serfontein. "I hope I'm still capable of a trip into town, and they haven't taken away my license yet. Besides, I had an appointment with my hairdresser and did not need to rush back."

She patted her beautifully coifed snow-white hair, which Jack correctly interpreted as a hint to compliment her.

"You look very elegant," he said obediently.

She twinkled at him, and he decided that he rather liked this formidable little lady.

Jack ushered her through to the room where he had interviewed Mma Nyembe a few days earlier. Despite her lack of inches she was an imposing woman, and he found himself marvelling at the similarities between her and Mma Nyembe, despite the obvious significant differences between them. Could it be just the age, he thought, or is it because these women survived times when it was difficult to be a woman.

"Your partner was asking me about my farm," she said, initiating the discussion, since Jack seemed to be lost in thought. "What's this all about? Why are you interested in Jakkalsvlei?"

"Yes, yes," answered Jack, concentrating on the present. "We traced the ownership of the farm from your father to you."

She nodded. "Yes, I inherited the farm when he died. By the time I inherited it, it was much smaller than the original farm. My father had already sold most of the land to my husband during the war. He kept just the main house, the vlei, and about two hundred hectares. That was what I inherited on his death."

"So, you were the only child then? You had no brothers or sisters?"

"Oh no, I had a brother. But he was disinherited before the war and I had no wish to see him again."

She looked grim for a second, and Jack wondered what had caused her frown.

"He was not a very nice person, my brother. My father disinherited him when he was twenty. He would not see him again or even allow him onto the farm."

Her lips pursed up when she spoke of her brother, as if there was a bad taste in her mouth. Obviously there was history there, thought Jack, one he might have to follow up on.

"My father lost everything because of Cobus," she continued, "which was why he needed to sell some of his land. I never heard the whole story – my father was a proud and private man, but I heard rumours that my brother ran off with all our father's money, leaving no one to help on the farm. Except for our young cousin, Hennie, that is."

"Hennie?" asked Jack, his ears pricking up at the name.

"Hennie. Hendrik van Tonder," said Nesta, as Joe and Jack flashed each other a triumphant grin. "He lived with us for about twelve years after his mother, my father's sister, died. He used to follow my brother around like a puppy, copying everything he did. He could not have chosen a worse role model."

Nesta looked sad. Some memories never fade, even after sixty years.

"What happened to Hennie?" asked Jack, trying hard to hide his elation.

"He ran away from home and joined the OB, becoming something of a local hero in the process."

"The OB? Do you mean the Ossewa Brandwag?"

"Yes. I think that was the only reason my father was willing to forgive him for walking out and leaving him without any help on the farm. In those days, it was quite an honour to have someone in your family in the Brandwag, especially, like Hennie, someone who was part of the Stormjaers."

"I don't think I've heard of the Stormjaers," said Jack, riveted by the history lesson. "Who were they?"

"I suppose you could call them the military wing of the OB," said Nesta. "The OB was mainly a peaceful cultural group, its members were ordinary Afrikaans men and women who wanted a homeland independent of the British. After the war, it became inconvenient to have what was considered a terrorist organisation linked to the new political elite. The group was dispersed and the members mostly joined the National Party, which eventually became the Nationalist government of South Africa. The rest you probably know."

Jack nodded. He was interested, but even more interested in the definite link between Van Tonder and Jakkalsvlei. His instinct had been right. There was definitely something very dodgy about that old man!

"So, what happened to Hennie? Where is he now?" Jack asked, although he was pretty sure he knew the answer.

"He lives right here, in Standerton. After the war, he joined the police force. He was pretty good at his job by the sounds of it. He was chief of police by the time he retired, about twenty years ago."

"What about your brother. What happened to him?"

"He turned up like the proverbial bad penny about seven years after the end of the war, having run through all of my father's money. He managed to persuade Hennie to find him a job with the police. As usual, he ruined it for himself, and almost ruined Hennie in the process."

"How do you know all this?" asked Jack.

"I'm old, not senile," she answered with a smile that took the sting out of the words. "It's a small town and I tend to hear everything."

"What happened?"

"He shot himself, a day after being bailed on murder and corruption charges. It was a bit of a family scandal, as Hennie was due to be the main witness at the trial. Some people are destined to cause trouble all their lives. Cobus was one of those."

Jack could not see any sadness in her face, only a matter-of-fact acceptance of the inevitability of retribution for the wicked. There was something very flinty in her eyes, and Jack guessed that she could tell him a lot more about Cobus Mostert if she was prompted.

Chapter 36

Joe was grinning like the cat that got the cream as Nesta Serfontein left the office. He felt that he had single-handedly cracked the case. Jack had to concede that Nesta Serfontein had provided them with an extraordinary amount of information in a very short space of time.

"This definitely links Van Tonder to the farm," Joe said triumphantly.

"Yes," answered Jack. "And if we look at the facts, we know that the children were abducted from Jakkalsvlei. We know that both Cobus Mostert and Hennie van Tonder lived at the farm. We also know that both names are on the title deed of the house, one as seller and the other as buyer."

"The problem is that Hennie only owned the house ten years later."

"Hmm," Jack frowned. "Perhaps the two men did it together. She said that Van Tonder followed his cousin around like a dog."

"They were policemen, though, and Van Tonder was a captain at the time of the murders. Would he risk his position for something like this?"

Joe shook his head, trying to get the pieces to fit.

"And a couple of years later, he was due to give evidence against his cousin in court. It doesn't sound as if they remained very good friends after the cousin returned."

"I think it's time we brought Van Tonder into the station for questioning," said Jack. "I want you to go to the retirement home and pick up the old man. Take one of the uniformed officers with in case he gives you trouble."

Joe was only too happy to do this, and within an hour he was triumphantly manoeuvring Van Tonder's wheelchair through the office.

Jack sat at the back of the large open-plan office, watching the arrival of the old man. He did not look at all worried about being there. Rather, he seemed interested in the station, taking a good look around, obviously comparing it to how it had looked when he was in charge. He seemed particularly interested in Jack's chalkboard with its notes about the case, and craned his neck around as he was wheeled past to try to read them.

Jack wondered for a moment if any of the officers would recognise him. But it had been at least twenty years since he retired. He doubted that any of the current staff were old enough to have been around in Van Tonder's day.

Chapter 37

1964

"Hey, boet! Why don't you come over and we can have some fun!"

Hennie's hackles rose as he heard his cousin's voice. Cobus was slurring his words. It was obvious that he was well into his second bottle of brandy.

"No, thanks," he said disdainfully. "Your idea of fun doesn't appeal to me. Besides, its Rick's birthday party and the house is full of children. I suggest you put down the bottle and sober up."

Hennie slammed down the telephone angrily. Every time Cobus had some 'fun', Hennie ended up cleaning up the mess. His previous warnings had made no impression on Cobus. By the sound of it, Cobus had picked up yet another prostitute and was making a party of the occasion. Definitely not Hennie's idea of a pleasant way to spend a Saturday afternoon.

Hennie shook his head at his wife, Hettie, mouthing the word 'Cobus'. She pursed her lips. She hated that man and could not understand why Hennie constantly bailed him out of whatever trouble he got himself into.

"Who wants ice cream?" shouted Hennie, and the children gathered around.

Soon, all thoughts of Cobus had been forgotten as the children enjoyed the games and treats. Little Elmarie struggled to keep up with her big brother and the older boys. She ended up spending the afternoon snuggled in her father's arms.

It was about nine that night when the next call came. Hettie picked up the phone and was tempted to drop it when she heard Cobus's voice. She was just about to put it down when Hennie popped his head around the corner, raising one eyebrow inquisitively.

"Cobus," she said in disgust, reluctantly handing over the phone. She had a feeling that this was going to be another unpleasant ending to an otherwise perfect day.

"Hennie, boet, I need your help," whispered Cobus into the phone.

"Speak up, man. I can't hear you," snapped Hennie. "Are you drunk again? For Christ's sake, I do have a family and a life to lead, you know!"

"Hennie, no, I'm not drunk. Well, yes, I suppose I am, but I need your help." It sounded as if Cobus was crying.

"No! We spoke about this last time, Cobus. I'm finished with tidying up your messes. Sort it out yourself."

"Hennie, please, the woman is dead. I think I've killed her. I need your help, boet. I really need your help."

Hennie froze. He tried to collect his thoughts, struggling to decide whether he should once again bail his cousin out of a disaster. He thought of his wife and his children, and his career.

"Hennie, you're the only person in the world who can help me. If it was me, you know, I'd help you. We're brothers," pleaded Cobus.

But I am never the one causing the trouble, thought Hennie to himself.

"I'm coming over, but you are going to solve this yourself. I'll be there in ten minutes."

Hettie had been listening to the one-sided conversation with rising fury. She launched into an angry tirade as Hennie put down the phone.

"You are never going to help him again!" she exclaimed incredulously.

"I will only be gone a short while. I'll be back as soon as I can. It is probably nothing, but I must just make sure he hasn't done anything stupid."

He eventually found the expensive new house in Charl Cilliers Street that Cobus had recently bought. A single light burned inside the lounge. Cobus was barefoot as he opened the door to Hennie. His bulging stomach hung over the top of a pair of khaki shorts, a sweaty vest barely covering his belly. He was flushed and sweating. A cigarette dangled from his listless fingers, the ash dropping unnoticed onto the entrance hall carpet.

"Hennie! Thank God you've come. The bloody woman just died under me. I didn't mean to kill her, I was just having some fun, and the next thing I knew she was dead."

"Show me," demanded Hennie.

Cobus stepped back to Hennie saw a scene of chaos in the lounge. The body of a slim young black woman lay on the couch, her arms tied with a nylon rope above her head and attached to the railing of the bar counter, a gag in her mouth.

Hennie's stomach churned. Memories of his childhood and the little black girl came rushing back to him. This was a thousand times worse. They weren't drunk teenagers anymore, they were police officers, and he at least prided himself on being a decent citizen, though he would not have applied the same epithet to his cousin.

"Where did this woman come from?" demanded Hennie. "Is this another prostitute?"

"No, she was trespassing on my father's farm. I picked her up there and thought I would have some fun before I sent her on her way. But she kept crying and screaming all the time. I thought she would get me into trouble, so I tied her up and gagged her."

"What were you doing on Oom Jaco's farm? He'd kill you himself if he saw you there. You're lucky he didn't come after you with his shotgun."

Hennie looked again at the girl.

"You are going to have to report this, Cobus. You can explain what happened, that you didn't intend to kill her, but you had obviously been raping her. And that is a crime."

"Raping a black girl! I will get off with a slap on the wrist," Cobus laughed sardonically. "But they will throw me off the force. This is the only job I know. You owe me! If I had not looked after you when we were boys, you would not have made it to puberty."

Hennie ignored him.

"Was she alone when you found her?" he asked.

Cobus looked shifty.

"No, not exactly," he answered. "There was another woman and some children. They are in the van."

"What are they doing in the van?" demanded Hennie, appalled.

"I didn't want them spoiling my fun," said Cobus sulkily.

"How long have they been there?"

"Since this morning," answered Cobus. "They'll be fine."

"Fine!" exclaimed Hennie, running outside. "Christ, it's been over thirty degrees today. It would have been much hotter than that in the van. You will be lucky if they have not all died from the heat!"

Hennie opened the door of the van. The stench from inside almost made him gag. In the dim reflected light from the house he could see various figures lying on the floor of the van. Not one was moving.

"Bring me a torch," he ordered.

Cobus lumbered heavily into the house and returned, carrying a powerful torch. Hennie reached for it and shone the beam of light into the dark interior of the van. The sight that was revealed was so horrifying that he almost dropped the torch.

"When did you say you brought them here?" he demanded in a whisper.

"This morning," said Cobus. Then he stopped to think. "No ... maybe it was yesterday morning."

Cobus peered into the interior of the van. The sight of the lifeless bodies seemed to surprise him.

"They were fine when I left them here," he muttered defensively.

"Help me get them out," demanded Hennie furiously. He leaned in to pick up the first small bundle. The child's lips were cracked and a swollen black

127

tongue protruded from her mouth. Hennie noticed that her body was covered in bruises and her arm appeared to be broken. She looked no more than eight or nine years old; more or less the same age as his little Elmarie.

He turned to Cobus with a look of horror on his face. He had no words to describe his feelings. One by one he took the children from the van, laying them down on the brick paving. There was one more body, that of a middle-aged woman. Her head was lying in a huge pool of blood, and she, too, was covered with bruises. Lying next to her was the knobkierrie that Cobus had used to beat them. It was covered with blood. Hennie took out his handkerchief, wrapped it around the knobkierrie and placed it next to the bodies.

"By my count, that is two women and seven children that you have managed to kill!"

"They are only kaffirs," said Cobus angrily. "Christ, what's wrong with you? Just help me carry them into the house. If you aren't prepared to help me, fine. I can do this on my own."

For a few moments Hennie looked at Cobus as if he was seeing him for the first time. Could this be his childhood hero? Had Cobus changed so much or was it he who had changed? Not finding an answer, he carried the children into the garage, laying them gently one by one. Finally, he carried through the older woman. Including the body inside, the total count was nine. Nine bodies.

As he finished, he turned to find Cobus leaning against the doorpost, watching him, his brandy bottle in his hand. Hennie was not a coward, but he knew Cobus, and he knew what he was capable of.

"You are going to have to deal with this yourself, Cobus," he said firmly. "This is one problem I am not going to help you with. I suggest you call the chief and explain yourself to him."

"And what do you think I am going to tell him? Do you think I'm going to take the blame for this all by myself?"

"What do you mean?" demanded Hennie angrily.

"Everyone knows you are my cousin. They know you and I are like this!" He held up two fingers, clenched together. "If they ask me I will tell them, how you and I were having our fun together. I will tell them that you brought them here. Their blood is all over your clothes."

"I have been with my family all weekend!" shouted Hennie, enraged. "Hettie will vouch for me."

"And wives have never lied for their husbands before?" mocked Cobus. "Even if they don't believe me completely, you will always be suspected, and you know what will happen to your promising career? Down the fucking toilet, boet! Down the fucking toilet."

Cobus laughed, the sound ending in a phlegmy cough.

Hennie stood, fists clenched, trying to stop himself launching into his massive cousin. His chances of survival if he did so were not very good, his slender frame being no match for Cobus's brute strength.

"Go home to your little boervrou and your little tjokkertjies. That little Elmarie is turning into a real beauty. She is just my type. You know the type I like, don't you, boet?" he smiled.

Hennie's barely controlled rage seemed to amuse him.

"Just go home and forget you saw anything here tonight. And if you think of saying anything, remember that your family are precious and dreadfully vulnerable. You wouldn't want anything to happen to them, would you?"

The threat was clear. Hennie had no illusions. Cobus would not hesitate to take his revenge on Hettie and the children if Hennie reported him to the police.

He turned his back on his cousin and walked out the door. He picked up the knobkierrie which was still lying on the bricks, and as he reached his car, he took off his shirt wrapping it around the bloody head of the knobkierie. Making a detour past the dump, he threw the knobkierrie, his shirt and his handkerchief into the incinerator.

Hettie was already asleep when he got home. He turned the shower up high and stood under it for a long, long time, feeling the hot water wash away the smell of blood and death. He wished he could wash the memory from his brain. But it was to haunt him for the rest of his life.

Chapter 38

2010

Jack entered the interview room where Van Tonder sat waiting, apparently relaxed and comfortable. His wheelchair was drawn up to the table, and he was looking around appreciatively.

"New furniture, I see," he said chattily. "We had ugly dark varnished tables and chairs when I was here, and the suspects had scratched their names into every available space; a real who's who of the criminal world of the day."

Jack was not quite sure how to tackle the former chief of police, but decided that one suspect was no different from another. He drew up his chair to the table and waited silently for Joe.

Joe arrived carrying some cool drinks. He put a Coke in front of Van Tonder and Jack.

"Never drink the stuff," said Van Tonder, "rots your teeth." He smiled, showing his yellowing teeth, several gaps bearing witness to departed comrades.

"Right, Mr van Tonder, you know the drill. We need to cover the essentials before we start."

"Fire away then. It'll be interesting to see what, if anything, has changed over the years."

"Please state your full name."

"Van Tonder. Hendrik Gerhard van Tonder."

"How old are you?"

"Too bloody old!"

"Mr van Tonder, please. We need this for the record. How old are you?"

"I'm eighty-nine years old."

"And where do you live?"

"I live at the Woodlands Retirement Home in Voortrekker Street, if you can call it living. More like a morgue, except the residents don't quite realise they're dead yet."

Jack's sense of humour was threatening to get the better of him. Although the old man was bloody annoying, he had a certain black humour about him.

"So, Mr van Tonder. Let's start with the house. You said you bought the house in 1974."

"No, I didn't. I said I owned it from 1974. There is a difference."

Jack frowned at him, irritated at this play on words.

"Okay, so you owned it from 1974. Who was the previous owner? The last time I spoke to you, you said you didn't know the owner."

"No, actually I said that the owner and the buyer of a property seldom meet, and that these transactions are usually dealt with by the agents and attorneys."

Jack's mouth was grim.

"Mr van Tonder, please. We're not here to play games. Do you know who the previous owner of that house was, prior to you 'owning' it?"

"Yes."

Jack clenched his teeth and asked with extreme patience.

"Who was the previous owner, before you owned it?"

"It was owned by Cobus Mostert."

Jack nodded to himself and made a note in his book.

"Now, correct me if I'm wrong. Cobus Mostert was your cousin. The two of you grew up together."

"Well, except for the fact that he was four years older than I was, which is a significant gap when you are young, yes. We grew up together on the farm; almost, you might say, like brothers. He left the farm when he was twenty."

"How old were you when you started living with your cousin's family?"

"I was almost eight years."

"So for ten years you lived with Cobus Mostert and his family."

"If you are interested in my family history, I would be happy to tell you all about it in more comfortable surroundings, maybe over a drink?"

Jack ignored the interruption.

"After he moved from the farm, when did you meet again?"

"We met a few times casually over the years, but he was living his life and I was living mine, and they were very different."

"And then you joined the police force here in 1946, is that correct?"

"You really seem to know all about me, Detective. Do you really need me here for this? I'm an old man and need my afternoon nap."

Jack went on, again ignoring Van Tonder. "From the sound of it, you had an interesting time during the war."

Although he had always been proud of his exploits with the Stormjaers during the war, Van Tonder had learnt that sometimes it was wise not to advertise the fact that he had been involved. He looked measuringly at Jack.

"We all did what we could to help our countrymen during that difficult time," he answered evasively.

Jack nodded. It was not an avenue he felt was relevant. He had simply wanted Van Tonder to be aware that he knew of his violent past.

"So, when did your cousin arrive back in Standerton?"

"I forget exactly. It was after my son was born. It must have been about 1952. He had been living in Bloemfontein and getting involved in the changing political scene."

"You must have been very happy to see him again, your childhood friend, because you got him a job in the police force."

Jack was surprised at the look of contempt on the old man's face.

"He applied and was accepted," said Van Tonder firmly. "I was not personally involved in offering him a job."

"But I am sure it helped his application that his brother was a rising star in the force, and a folk hero as well."

"He was not my brother," spat Van Tonder.

"Well, as good as a brother," said Jack, conceding the point. "You spent your childhood under the same roof. You probably shared a bedroom as children." Jack was beginning to enjoy himself. It was rapidly becoming obvious that Van Tonder had no great love for his cousin.

Van Tonder muttered something angrily under his breath.

"What was that?" asked Jack. "I missed it."

"I said a bedroom would have been nice. We slept on mattresses, thin roll-up mattresses, on the stoep, summer and winter, with just a thin blanket to cover us. We wore the same clothes, day and night until they fell off our backs. We worked from sunrise to sundown seven days a week, until our hands bled and our muscles ached. Hardly the sort of comfort you grew up in, I'm sure!"

Jack had been in a rhythm, not paying too much attention to the subtleties of Van Tonder's replies. But his last remark made him look up from his notes and observe the old man more piercingly. Just because a man was white did not mean he had had an easy life. I'm making an assumption about the man, he thought with shame, based on my own prejudice. I am making judgements based on his colour. It was something that he despised, and now was personally guilty of. He tried to imagine the sort of life Van Tonder had lived; obviously a hard life, one that would either have turned men into brothers, or enemies.

"So, Cobus lived here from his arrival in 1952 until his death in 1973. During those years, did you spend much time together? Did your families socialise?"

"In the beginning we did, but I was married and my life revolved around my wife and children, and my job of course. Cobus never married. He lived the life of a bachelor."

"You sound as if you didn't approve of his lifestyle," suggested Jack.

"It wasn't my business to approve or disapprove. We lived our separate lives. We saw each other at work, and once in a while we would see each other after work for a drink or a game of rugby, but we did not socialise."

"What made you buy his house?"

"I have already told you twice. I did not buy his house."

"You must have done. I have a title deed with your name on it."

"You need to do your homework more thoroughly, Detective. Look carefully at that title deed. It gives the previous owner as the deceased estate of Jacobus Johannes Mostert. I inherited the property. After he died, I found that he had left it to me."

"If you were no longer close, why would he have left you the house?" Jack was sure he was close to an answer here.

"I suppose it was his idea of a bad joke," muttered Van Tonder sourly under his breath. Then he said louder, "I was his only relative, except for his sister whom he hadn't seen since he left the farm. I suppose he had no one else to leave it to."

Jack looked at him for a long time. He needed to do a little more digging. Turning to Joe, he indicated that he was bringing the interview to a close.

"Detective Bantu will be taking you back to the retirement home. I don't suppose you are a flight risk so I won't be leaving a constable there. Please make sure you are available on Monday morning at ten for collection."

"I look forward to it," answered Van Tonder breezily. "This is the most interesting day I've had since my accident!"

Heading out of the station for lunch, Jack nearly collided with Thuli, who was running up the stairs.

He reached out and caught her as she lost her balance, his head spinning with the excitement of holding her in his arms. He released her self-consciously and was further embarrassed to find her smiling at his obvious discomfort.

"I came to invite you to come over to my house for a drink this evening. It's my first day back in the house and I wanted to thank you for the excellent job your people have done to clean up and repair the damage. Also, Katie and Patrick are here and I thought, since you know Patrick, you might like the chance to meet up with him again."

Thuli had thought long and hard about the invitation. She didn't want to look desperate but had taken an uncharacteristic liking to Jack. And he was being really elusive. She had never found any man whose company she enjoyed so much, and had been hoping he would make the first move. Since this was not happening, some intervention was required. Katie's visit to town seemed to offer the ideal opportunity.

"That sounds like a great idea. We weren't exactly friends, Patrick and I. He was more like my nemesis. We played for different teams, and his team always seemed to beat us."

"Well, have you gotten over your disappointment?" she laughed. "If not, it could be a very awkward evening."

"Oh, on the contrary it would be great to meet up with him again. And from what I hear of her, Katie sounds very nice. So yes, I would love to come. What time?"

"Around six? We'll just have some drinks and snacks. Nothing fancy. Very casual."

"You've got it," he smiled.

"By the way, I heard you arrested Katie's grandfather. Is it true?" she asked.

"How do these bloody stories get out?" he demanded. "No. The answer is no, I have not arrested Mr van Tonder. In fact, I've just sent him back to the retirement home after a very interesting discussion. He'll be returning on Monday to help us further with our enquiries."

"Help us further with our enquiries," Thuli mocked. "That sounds like cop talk for 'we have arrested the miserable old bastard'."

"Actually, I've started developing a strange liking for him. What on earth did he do to you to make you hate him so much?" Jack asked in bemusement.

"Try to imagine that you are a little girl of say eight years old. You are at your best friend's grandmother's house having a tea and cake and playing hide and seek. You find a wonderful spot behind some boxes in the garage, waiting with great anticipation for your friend to find you. Then suddenly, out of the blue, this crazy old man grabs you by the arm, screaming like a banshee, and hurls you physically out of the house."

"What on earth had you done?" Jack asked, laughing.

"Nothing, I swear. And it is really not funny! I'd never really seen him that often before. When I did, there had been no problems, and I'd certainly not done anything that might upset him. I was just playing with my friend. It took me years to get over the terror of that day. For a long time, every time I saw a white man I used to run and hide. And every time I passed that house after that day, I used to run as fast as I could, hoping that man would not see me."

"Wow, you poor thing! It sounds as if the incident really affected you!" Jack started to smile sympathetically, but suddenly his face changed. "I wonder," he mused, looking at her with narrowing eyes.

"What?" she demanded, catching his look.

"I must go!" he said with a quick smile. "See you later!" And with that, he ran to his car and was gone.

Wills are public records, and it took Jack just half an hour to locate the correct document and check the details. Cobus Mostert had died with only one real asset – his house. He had no investments, no large cash balances and no insurances. His house was insured and mortgage free, and had been left to his cousin, Hendrik Gerhard van Tonder. Jack checked the date of the will. It was made in February 1963, just three months before the murders. Unless they were involved in it together, would Mostert really still have left his cousin the house? It seemed unlikely.

A copy of the will in his briefcase, he returned to the station. He was interested in the case against Mostert back in the day, in which his cousin was supposed to give testimony. He was also interested in the suicide. Had a note been left? How had Mostert committed suicide?

The file was not in the cabinet. Instead, there was a faded piece of paper saying that it was a restricted file. Jack looked thoughtfully at the sheet of paper. Restricted? Why? It was time he talked to the chief. He went through to Webster's office, arriving just in time to see him putting a golf ball neatly into a cup at the other end of his office. Webster was one of the older officers and was happily loafing his way through his last six months of work until retirement.

Jack's request for a restricted file on Mostert was not questioned, until Jack mentioned the name of Hendrik van Tonder.

Webster straightened up, for the first time giving Jack his full attention.

"Van Tonder? Why do you want a file on Van Tonder? He was a bloody fine officer. I served under him when I was a young man, you know."

Jack was quick to see that he might have played his cards badly.

"Actually, it is the file on Cobus Mostert I was looking for, not Van Tonder. I just wanted to find out the details of the investigation that was being carried out in the months before his suicide. It has to do with the bodies we found in the house he used to own."

"Mostert!" spat Webster. "That scum. He would have spent a lifetime in prison if he had not shot his brains out. As things turned out, he saved the taxpayer a fortune. He was up for prostitution, extortion, rape, drug dealing, weapons smuggling ... you name it. He was even suspected of several murders. Hennie van Tonder and I had been investigating him for about a year, and we had a mountain of evidence.

"Then we arrested him early one morning, got him out of bed with some girl. And then the bloody magistrate bailed him pending trial. If anyone should have been locked up to prevent further mayhem, it was Mostert. Two days later he shot himself." He chipped the next ball neatly into the cup. "It couldn't have happened to a more deserving guy."

He walked over to a cabinet in a corner of his office and unlocked it, selecting a file that he handed over to Jack. "It really does not need to be restricted anymore. The guy has been dead for nearly forty years."

Clutching the file, Jack made his escape.

Chapter 39

Jack felt very strange going into Thuli's house. Up to now it had been a crime scene, and here he was entering it socially. Thuli greeted him at the door, unexpectedly giving him a quick kiss on the mouth. He was glad it was quite dark so she did not see that she had caught him unawares. He could hear voices from the patio. He followed Thuli through the house to be introduced to Katie and Patrick.

If Patrick did not recognise him, you would not have known it. He slapped Jack's shoulder and claimed that Jack's team had been their biggest challenge when he was still on the school team. Jack had been prepared to be faced with a prima donna with a huge ego, but was pleasantly surprised to find that Patrick had not changed from being the quiet unassuming guy he had always been. He did find it difficult to adjust to the slight English accent in Patrick's voice, but they were soon catching up on local gossip about old friends.

Katie and Thuli were relieved that the two men seemed to like each other. They had half a year's worth of news to catch up on, not least the discovery of the bodies in this very house, and the implication that Katie's grandfather appeared to be involved in the matter in some way.

After catching up on their own news, Thuli and Katie started pumping Jack none too gently to try to find out some more about the progress of the investigation, specifically whether he thought that Van Tonder was involved in the killings.

"We promise not to tell anyone," they pleaded.

Patrick gently stepped in to support Jack. "Jack's quite right not to talk about the case," he said, "especially since he's your grandfather, Katie. That could really compromise any case that is eventually brought. You wouldn't like that, now would you?"

Patrick's quiet good sense prevailed and the women allowed the subject to drop. The rest of the evening was spent chatting about their very different lives, and listening to some music the couple had brought Thuli from London. It was very late when Katie and Patrick left. Thuli held firmly onto Jack's arm as he made to follow them, preventing him from leaving.

"Do you have anywhere particular you need to be right now?" she asked with a smile as she slipped her arms around his back.

"Tonight? No, I'm definitely not on duty."

"That's a pity," she whispered into his ear. "I was hoping you could protect me, this being my first night alone in the house again since it became a crime scene. I'm a little nervous to be here on my own."

Jack knew that a sensible man would have walked out the door. However, he found that he was not a sensible man.

Chapter 40

1973

As Hennie came down the stairs from the magistrate's court, he saw Cobus surrounded by a group of hangers-on and two reporters.

"So, now that you are out on bail," a busty blonde was asking, "what are you going to do until your court date in April?"

"Well," answered Cobus, observing his cousin's progress down the stairs. "I thought I'd go out and get me some company and have a little fun! There's my dear cousin who is going to be a witness against me at my trial," he sneered. "Now, he knows exactly my type! He knows just the kind of girl I like."

Hennie curled his fists. Above all things, he needed to keep his cool. Reacting to Cobus's taunts could bring the whole case down, and this was something he and young Webster had been working on for eighteen months.

He was aware that Cobus was not a man to be crossed, but his cousin's exploits had been getting more and more blatant, taunting him, daring him to do something about it. Hennie's frustration had finally boiled over. He knew he would be risking everything to stop Cobus's reign of terror, but he could no longer allow it to go on.

Above all, he wanted to end the stranglehold that Cobus held over him. He had planned the whole operation carefully and thought he had everything under control. But then the magistrate had unexpectedly granted Cobus bail. Hennie had a bad feeling about this, sure that Cobus was plotting his revenge.

Hennie was still angry when he arrived home. Hettie had left a cold supper out for him as she had gone to bed early to show her displeasure. She knew what Cobus was capable of, and she was furious with Hennie for risking his family and his career by going after him.

He sat down alone at the kitchen table and looked at the cold meal. Even if it had looked more appetising, he simply could not face eating. He leaned down and placed the plate on the floor, where it was gratefully accepted by the dog.

He dropped his head onto his hands, running his fingers across his temples and into his hair. His hatred for Cobus threatened to overwhelm him. More than anything, he wished his father had left him with any other family in the world.

Hettie's head was turned away from him as she lay in their bed. Hennie went around to her side of the bed and placed his hand on her shoulder.

"Hettie, please listen to me. I must talk to you. This is very important."

Hettie pretended for a moment that she had not heard him, that she was asleep, but the urgency in his voice finally made her relent.

"What is it?" she demanded angrily.

"Hettie, I'm afraid. I'm afraid that Cobus will go after Elmarie."

"He wouldn't dare!" she gasped in dismay.

"That's the problem," answered Hennie, "I think he might. Last time I refused to help him out of a disaster he more or less threatened to rape her."

Hettie looked at him in horror.

"You didn't tell me that!" she whispered.

"Today when I was leaving court he pretty much implied the same thing. We have got to keep Elmarie home from school tomorrow and then on Friday I'll drop the two of you at your brother's house in Welkom until he is back in prison."

"She is busy writing exams. She has to go to school until the end of the term. We can't keep her away! Not without some very good reason."

He longed to tell her what Cobus was capable of, to tell her something of the darker side of their history. But he feared how she would react if she knew what he had done when he was a boy, and what he had allowed Cobus to get away with over the years. He didn't want her image of him to be tainted by events he had tried to put behind him decades ago.

"Well, in that case, we had better make sure that we drop her and fetch her from school, and that there is always somebody with her."

"This is all your fault!" she exclaimed angrily. "Why did you have to go after him like this? You know exactly what he is like. He can bring down your career and land you in jail right next to him. If you knew that Elmarie was at risk, why were you determined to stand in court and testify against him? Why? Why couldn't you just let it go?"

"Hettie, a time comes in a man's life when he can't stand back anymore; when he has to take that risk and stand up for what is right. I just couldn't live with myself anymore."

"But what about us?" she cried. "What about me and your children? Are we not worth living for?"

"I wish I could make you understand," he said sadly. "I just have to do what is right."

Hennie left for work early in the morning, secure in the knowledge that Hettie was taking Rick and Elmarie to school. He spent the day in a state of nervous tension, drinking a dozen cups of coffee, unable to concentrate on his work. He was due to pick up Elmarie at school at two-thirty, but by one-thirty he was already out of the door. He arrived at the school and ran up the few steps to the entrance. The principal was just passing through the doors.

"Ah, Mr van Tonder, you are too late," she smiled. "Your charming cousin has already picked up Elmarie. He said he was taking her to the hospital. I hope your wife will be alright?"

Hennie gaped at her in horror. "My cousin, when did he fetch her?"

"About twenty minutes ago," she answered. She saw the look of horror on Hennie's face, and panicked.

"I hope I did the right thing, allowing her to go. He said your wife had fallen and you had taken her to hospital."

But Hennie did not stop to answer. He was running for his car.

He arrived at Cobus's house in less than five minutes. Despite the urgency, he took the time to park his car a block away, out of sight of the house, hoping to rely on the element of surprise. He went through the metal gate which hung by a single hinge. Once on the property, he was hidden by the untended wilderness of the garden. He had only once been into the house itself very fleetingly, so he was in unfamiliar territory.

Quietly, gun in hand, he tried the front door, but it was locked. He ran at a crouch around the house towards the back. Fortunately, there was no dog to warn of his arrival. He peeped around the corner. Nothing! The back garden contained a rusty braai and was littered with rubbish.

He walked carefully towards the window, and took a quick look into the room. It was the sitting room. He could see Elmarie, lying on the floor next to the built-in bar. Her hands were tied with electric cable and attached above her head to the rail of the bar. Her mouth was filled with some sort of cloth. Her face was streaked with tears and her eyes were wide with fear. Hennie looked around the room and tried to see down the passage.

There was no sign of Cobus. Hennie tapped softly on the window. Elmarie looked up and saw him. Her eyes widened with hope. He placed his finger on his lips and shook his head gently. She nodded, and then looked pointedly down towards the passage.

Hennie tried the patio door, but it was also locked. Quietly he ran around the house and found a third entrance, a back door into the garage. This time he was in luck. The handle turned quietly, and he carefully pushed open the door and entered the garage closing the door behind him. Except for Cobus's black Ford Escort, the garage was empty. It was the first time he had been there since that horrible night, four years earlier. It brought back terrible memories of the bodies he had carefully placed exactly where he was standing. To this day he wondered how Cobus had disposed of the bodies, and wrestled with his conscience about his silence on that day. Just look where his actions had brought him. Quietly, he moved through the garage and into the kitchen where he could hear Cobus prattling on menacingly.

"Hey, sweet Elmarie, pretty little Elmarie. You and I are going to have a little fun! Do you like to have fun? Look at me when I'm talking to you, dammit! Do you know why we are going to have fun? We are going to have fun because your self-righteous bloody father is having his fun at my fucking expense. He thinks he can put me in jail. Well, he is going to learn differently. If he wants to play, that's fine. I love playing. You just need to know that whatever happens here today is not my fault. It is your father's fault. His touching moral outrage is obviously more important to him than his daughter and his family! He is going to regret the day he decided to betray me. He is going to have to live with this for the rest of his life."

His voice was slurred. Obviously, he was deep into the brandy bottle already. Hennie was relieved, as this would slow down his reactions. He took off his shoes and left them in the kitchen. Then he slowly advanced down the passage towards the sitting room. He could see Elmarie's panic-stricken face, and Cobus's back.

Cobus's attention was totally focused on Elmarie as he unzipped and dropped his trousers around his ankles, cradling his penis in his hands.

"Have you seen one of these before?" he asked with a leer. He bent down towards the frightened girl, completely unaware of Hennie behind him, until something in Elmarie's eyes warned him. He turned, but he was too late. Hennie grabbed him, one arm crooked tightly around his neck, while his other hand twisted Cobus's arm up behind him, making him scream in agony.

Cobus reeled around the room, trying to shake Hennie off, but Hennie's rage had given him a strength he would otherwise have lacked. Cobus was at a disadvantage, his trousers tripping him as he fought to throw Hennie off his back. He landed hard, and Hennie sat astride his back. He reached into his back pocket and pulled out his handcuffs. He fastened Cobus's hands together and then tied him to the bar rail where Elmarie was still imprisoned, taking care to avoid Cobus's legs as he thrashed about. Cobus was screaming curses, his face red with rage.

Hennie removed the gag from Elmarie's mouth and thrust it firmly into Cobus's. He then untied his daughter and gently helped her to her feet.

With rescue came relief, and Elmarie threw herself into her father's arms, sobbing hysterically.

"Are you alright?" he asked anxiously, quickly leading her out of the house through the back garden.

She nodded bravely through her tears.

"I'm fine, Dad," she said. "He frightened me, but you got here just in time. I think he is mad. He looked mad enough to kill someone."

He stopped her, holding her face between his hands and concentrating her attention on what he had to say.

"Elmarie, I want you to do something for me. This is very important. Your life and mine might depend on it."

She nodded, her eyes wide.

"I am going to drop you off at home now. Stay in your room until I come back. I don't want you to talk to anyone, not anyone. Do you understand?"

She nodded. "What about Mom?" she asked.

"Especially not her!" her father exclaimed. "This is going to be a secret between you and me, forever. Remember that. Your mother must never know. You are never to talk to another soul about this day, as long as you live."

"Okay, Dad," she whispered. "I promise."

Hennie returned to the house immediately. He went into the sitting room to find Cobus straining to pull his fat fists through the handcuffs. His eyes pleaded for mercy, but Hennie was not feeling merciful. He remembered the day he and Oom Jaco had found the chief lying dead in the workers' village. He should have known then that this man was evil, but he was so devoted to his handsome cousin that he allowed himself to be blind to his faults. It had taken him years to break free from the allegiance he had felt; an allegiance to someone who did not deserve it. For the first time since Cobus had returned to Standerton, Hennie felt that he was in control of his own destiny. This time he needed to deal with the problem properly. This time he needed to end it.

He made an educated guess as to where Cobus kept his service revolver and was relieved to find it where he expected it to be. Cobus watched him with increasing fear, his bare feet trying to find a foothold, his hands desperately trying to free themselves from the cuffs.

Hennie felt calmer than he had felt in a long time. He felt no remorse; no pity.

"I think it's time to put an end to this situation, don't you agree?" he asked conversationally.

Cobus shook his head desperately, his pleas muffled by the gag, the sweat dripping down his chin and staining his shirt. Hennie wrinkled his nose at the smell of alcohol and sweat mingled with urine – a particularly pungent aroma.

He picked up a pillow from the couch with which to deaden the noise and limit the mess. Without a word, he placed the gun against Cobus's right temple, then stopped, dropping his hand. Cobus breathed a sigh of relief. Hennie stepped back and looked at Cobus and then around the room, considering all alternatives.

But Hennie had not changed his mind. He had just remembered that Cobus was left-handed. He moved around, placing the gun to his cousin's left temple, taking his time to make sure the shot would enter at exactly the correct angle.

"Goodbye, boetie," he said simply, and pulled the trigger. Cobus's body jerked once, then lay still.

Despite the cushion there was a lot of blood. Hennie was pleased that the floor was tiled with plastic tiles – they would be relatively easy to clean. He spent the next couple of hours setting the scene. He had seen enough suicides to know exactly how everything should look.

It was already dusk when Hennie left the way he had come, first making sure that no one was around to see him.

First he dropped the cloths, his shirt and the bloody cushion into the incinerator at the dump. Then he went home.

Elmarie was asleep, looking like the innocent young teenager that she was. He sat at the edge of the bed and tucked a soft curl behind her ear. She awoke, a question in her eyes.

"He will never frighten you again, my darling," said her father.

She smiled sleepily. "It is our secret," she said, and drifted back to sleep.

Chapter 41

2010

Jack awoke in an unfamiliar bed with the sound of dishes in the kitchen and the smell of coffee drifting up the stairs. Remembering the previous night, he smiled contentedly. He couldn't believe that this amazing woman who he had been dreaming about for weeks felt the same way about him. He heard the sound of her bare feet on the stairs, then saw her framed in the doorway with the light behind her. He felt he was quite possibly the luckiest man in the world.

Thuli placed the two cups on her nightstand and climbed back into bed with him. Holding out his arms, he drew her into a fierce hug, burying his face in her hair. She squeaked, and he released her.

"Sorry, a little too tight?" he asked playfully.

"Actually, I rather like a good strong hug," she teased. "Are you ready for some coffee?"

"Coffee first, and then let's see if last night was just a fluke, or if we are made for each other."

"Hmm, sounds like a plan," she whispered into his ear, sliding her arm around his waist, "how do you feel about cold coffee?"

He laughed happily. "I think I can live with it."

It was some time later when they finally managed to drink their coffee, which Thuli had quickly run through the microwave.

When the phone rang they looked at each other ruefully before Thuli reached out to answer it. It was Katie, and she was crying.

"Wait, start again," said Thuli, "I can't hear a word you are saying ... what is it about your father?"

"He had another stroke," answered Katie tearfully. "He didn't make it."

"Oh Katie, I'm very sorry," said Thuli. "Where are you? Would you like me to come over?"

"Would you? I'm at home with my mom. She's taken it very badly. She hasn't said a single word since they called. You know, for the past ten years I have hated him, and now all I can remember are the good things. I feel so bad. I have been awful to him. I haven't even visited him in hospital since I got married. He was a good man. Very humourless, perhaps, and maybe he went about things the wrong way, but he was a good man who cared about me."

"I'll let my boss know I won't be coming in today. Give me half an hour."

As Thuli left to comfort her friend, Jack headed for the retirement home. It all seemed wrong to him. Rick van Tonder had seemed to be growing stronger, and now without warning he was dead. He did not like it when things seemed wrong.

He drove up to Woodlands, parking next to a hearse which had just arrived. Hendrik van Tonder was sitting in his wheelchair at his son's bedside as the nurses prepared the body to be removed by the men from the mortuary. He refused to move out of the way, so they had to work around him. There was no joking about, and no one referred to him as Umkhulu. They could see that the old man was in a state of misery, and they looked on sympathetically, speaking quietly amongst themselves in Zulu.

For all the attention he paid to them, they could have been shouting and dancing. Van Tonder was completely oblivious to his surroundings, his attention concentrated on the pale and motionless figure of his only son. He was remembering Rick's birthday party. The ice cream melting in the cones ... the sheepdog ... what was his name again ... licking up anything that fell to the floor.

He remembered little Elmarie, her blonde curls and her shy smile as she held out plump arms for a cuddle. She had never been the same again after Cobus's death. Hennie had taken a long time to realise that the secret she was keeping was eating away at her, killing her from within. She was just twenty one when she jumped from the bridge over the Vaal River and was carried away in an instant.

Hennie's guilt and remorse were more than he could bear, made worse because they irrevocably changed the relationship between himself and his wife.

Hettie was no fool. She must have known that Cobus's death was too convenient to be a coincidence. Looking back, she must also have known that Elmarie had, in some way, been involved.

Yet after Elmarie's death, Hettie had put up a brave front. She smiled and socialised. She cared for her son and then her granddaughter, Katie. She never once gave any indication that Elmarie's death had killed something in her too. The love between Hennie and Hettie that had been so strong for so many years became a mask – a façade she maintained for her family. Then, ten years after Elmarie's suicide to the day, Hettie followed her into the Vaal River.

The tears coursed down the old man's wrinkled face, dripping unchecked from his trembling chin.

As Jack entered the room, the spell was broken, and Hennie clutched the detective's sleeve.

"I killed him," he croaked hoarsely, almost hysterical, "I killed my boy. First, I killed Elmarie, and then I killed Hettie, and now my son. Take me away! Lock me up and throw away the key. I can't stand it anymore. I can't stand it."

Hennie sobbed, deep gasping sobs that shook his old thin frame.

Jack looked enquiringly at the nurses. They shook their heads. He jerked his head at the matron, who followed him out into the corridor.

"What does he mean, he killed his son?" asked Jack.

"He came in this morning and spent about half an hour speaking with Mr Rick. I was here in the nurse's station and I could see him as clearly as now, but I couldn't hear what he was saying. There was a monitor attached to Mr Rick's arm and I could see that his heart rate was increasing, which gave me cause for concern. But Umkhulu definitely didn't do anything to kill his son, I swear it. He was sitting at least a metre away from the bed the whole time."

"So what does he mean by saying he killed him?" asked Jack in exasperation.

"My guess is that whatever it was that he was saying to his son was so terrible that it caused Mr Rick to have another stroke."

Jack looked through the glass at where the old man sat slumped in his chair. He was no longer the jaunty, cheeky figure of yesterday with the easy repartee. Hennie van Tonder was a broken man.

"Is he well enough to be taken to the station?" Jack asked.

"Is that really necessary?" the nurse asked in reply.

"Considering the confession he has just made, I have little choice. I've a duty to investigate, and I have to question him properly."

"Would it not be possible to do it here?" she asked. "At least that way we could be on hand to take care of him if it is too much for him. We have a room where you can be completely private. I promise you'll not be disturbed."

"Give me an hour to set it up," he said, pulling out his phone. Quickly, he spoke to Joe. Then he called the chief, who was halfway through a game of golf. At first Webster was inclined to be angry with Jack for upsetting his old friend, but once he heard the facts, promised to drop everything and come to the retirement home. It sounded as if the old man would need a friend.

Chapter 42

The meeting room at the retirement home was far more comfortable than the interview room at the station. Webster and Joe sat quietly to one side, Joe monitoring the recording equipment, Webster observing. Van Tonder sat motionless in his wheelchair with Jack facing him, a notebook in front of him on a small table.

"This is a continuation of our interview of yesterday," said Jack. "For the record, can we reconfirm your name."

"Hendrik van Tonder," said the old man dully.

"Mr van Tonder, earlier this morning you said you had killed your son, and that you had also killed your daughter and your wife. Is that correct?"

Hennie nodded. He then cleared his throat loudly and said, "Ja. Ja, that is correct."

"What did you mean by that? What did you mean by saying you killed them?"

"I may not have plunged a knife into their hearts, or shot them, or pushed them into the water, but in real terms I was the one who caused their deaths, each and every one of them."

Jack sat back in his chair and looked at his chief.

"Hennie," said Webster kindly. "You and I are mates from the old days. I know exactly how Elmarie and Hettie died, and you certainly weren't responsible for their deaths. On each occasion, you were working far away. In fact, when Hettie died you and I were in Germiston following that suspect in that drug distribution ring, remember?"

"There are many ways of killing people," shouted Hennie. "I know! I have killed a few in my time. The worst way to kill someone is to kill them slowly from the inside."

"I think it's time you told us the full story," said Jack.

"How much time have you got?" said Hennie with a deep sigh. "This goes back a long, long way."

"I don't have any other plans or dates for today. We have all the time in the world. You just take your time and tell the story in your own words."

The sun was setting as Hennie finished telling his story. A few dried-out sandwiches lay uneaten on a tray, and coffee mugs and water glasses littered the table. To Jack, the world of the old man's story was a totally different one to the world in which he had grown up. Most of the pivotal events had happened before he was even born.

Hendrik van Tonder fell silent. His story had ended. After a few minutes in which they all sat still, absorbing the disasters and tragedies that had befallen this family, Jack indicated for Joe to turn off the video camera.

Jack stood up, straightening his stiff back. The events of the morning and the previous night seemed to stretch out forever. He thought he would never feel the same about anything again.

The old man held out his hands, wrists together.

"Now, are you going to arrest me?" he asked quietly.

Jack looked at Webster.

"I think you will be safe enough here," said the chief. "It's late and we are all tired. We can pick up again tomorrow."

Jack opened the door and stepped out of the room. He saw the matron sitting on a sofa in front of the television. She got heavily to her feet as she saw that they had finally come to the end of their interview.

"How is Umkhulu?" she asked quietly.

"He is pretty exhausted, but I think he'll be more at peace now. Could you please keep an eye on him? I think he could be a suicide risk."

She looked concerned.

"Mr Rick's room has been cleared and is ready. I will place him there for the night," she said. "It's not ideal to put him in his dead son's bed, but unfortunately it's the only one available where I can keep an eye on him through the night."

"We'll be back first thing in the morning," promised Jack.

As he left Woodlands, he switched on his phone. There were three missed calls from Thuli. He dialled her number.

"Jack, I have been trying to call you all day," she sounded relieved. "Where have you been? I hope you haven't been trying to fob me off after last night."

"Definitely not!" he replied. "I am sorry. I have just been tied up all day with a very difficult case. I turned off my phone because I could not be disturbed."

"What was it about?" she asked. "Is it something you can talk about?"

"Not tonight," he said wearily. "I will call you tomorrow morning."

"Aren't you coming over tonight?" Thuli asked tentatively.

"No, not tonight," he said. "I am totally exhausted. Besides, I honestly don't think I would be great company. This has been the most difficult case of my life. I need time to think it through, and for that I need to be alone."

"Oh!" she said in a small voice.

"Thuli, please don't take this the wrong way. I think you're the best thing that has ever happened to me. But tonight I need to be alone. Please try to understand. If we're going to have any sort of relationship, you will need to understand that I am first and foremost a policeman, and that my job will sometimes place tremendous strain on me. Sometimes, I'll just need to be alone."

"Take all the time you need," Thuli said. Jack could hear the relief in her voice. "And when you are ready for company, you know where to find me."

He snapped his phone shut and headed for the office. Before he went to bed, there was one thing he wanted to check.

The station office was deserted, everyone either off duty or out on some mission. He unlocked his filing cabinet and took out the Vilikazi file. Something was ringing a bell in his head and he needed to be sure he was right.

And there it was. The investigating officer in the Vilikazi case was Cobus Mostert, with Hennie as the senior officer. Then he picked up Hector Vilikazi's notebook. That word that had bothered him – 'most' – if that word was read as 'Mostert', the whole case made sense. It would also mean that the mystery of Hector's death in an alleyway was solved. In all likelihood, Hector had been getting too close to the truth of what had happened to his wife and the children. Most likely, Cobus Mostert had dealt with it in his usual callous way.

Jack thought of Hennie's confession, of how he had shot Cobus and covered it up to look like suicide. While he could never condone murder, there was a sense here of justice having been done. Satisfied, he locked the file back into his desk and left for home.

It had taken Jack a long time to unwind when he got home, and when his phone rang he felt as if he had just fallen asleep. The alarm clock glowing next to his bed showed three o'clock. He cursed as he fumbled for his phone.

"Malepo," he mumbled, fighting to clear his head.

"Detective, this is the Matron Marjorie from Woodlands."

That focused his attention fast.

"I'm sorry to wake you in the middle of the night. I thought you would want to know right away. Mr van Tonder passed away in his sleep about ten minutes ago, at exactly two forty-five am."

"Oh shit! Sorry Mma, I mean, thanks for letting me know," said Jack, rubbing his head, trying to clear the cobwebs from his mind. "Is there anything you think I need to deal with right now, or can I come over in the morning?"

"Detective, he was an old man who went through too much in a few short months. He died as we all do in the end. There's nothing you can do for him now. There's nothing any of us can do for him. He's in God's hands now. Go back to sleep and I'll see you in the morning."

Her motherly advice made sense. Jack sent a text message to Joe to meet him at Woodlands at nine the next morning, set his alarm, and dropped into a dreamless sleep.

It seemed that everyone was at Woodlands when he arrived there a few short hours later. Julie and Thuli had gone through to deal with the paperwork relating to the two deaths in as many days. Katie was pale. It was obvious that the strain was proving too much for her. Patrick stood behind her, looking uncomfortable and out of place. He looked relieved when he saw Jack.

"Did you hear that my grandfather has also died?" asked Katie sadly.

"Yes, I'm very sorry for your loss," Jack answered.

"There is one thing that I want to know, and I want you to give me an honest answer. One of the nurses said that my grandfather killed my father. Is that true? Did that horrible old bastard kill my father?"

"No! No, definitely not," said Jack emphatically. "Your father died of a stroke, just as the matron said."

"Then why would my grandfather say he killed him; and my grandmother; and my aunt Elmarie? Why would he say that if it wasn't true?"

"Just take my word for it. He did not kill your father. And he did not kill your grandmother, or your aunt. Your father died of a stroke, and your grandmother committed suicide on the tenth anniversary of her daughter's suicide."

"I don't believe you!" Katie shouted, a tinge of hysteria in her voice. "I have always suspected him of killing my grandmother, and now I know the truth!"

She dropped into the closest chair, sobbing hysterically, while Patrick unsuccessfully tried to calm her.

Jack kneeled down in front of her.

"Katie, listen to me! When your grandmother died, your grandfather was in Germiston with my chief, three hundred and fifty kilometres from where she jumped off the bridge. She left a suicide note which is on file in the evidence store at the police station."

"I don't understand. It just doesn't make any sense at all," sobbed Katie. "All I know is that my father is dead, and my grandfather too. It's just too much."

Jack was relieved to see Thuli and Julie come down the passage from the matron's office. Thuli threw him a shy smile and knelt down next to Katie, taking her into her arms and rocking her, singing comforting words into Katie's ear. After a few minutes, the sobbing eased and Katie showed a woeful face.

"I'm sorry about that. I'm not usually a hysterical person, but I really do need to know what happened," she said, ashamed.

"Thuli, why don't you take them all to your house? Give me half an hour to sort things out here, and I'll join you. And then, Katie, I promise to tell you everything, and I promise not to leave out any detail."

It was more like an hour before Jack joined them. Against regulations, he had decided to bring along the evidence tape, and had made a detour past the station to pick it up. He would certainly not be showing all of it – it was more than five hours long. But there were certain parts of the story which he thought would be better told in the words of the old man.

He was not surprised to see that Mma Nyembe had joined them. It seemed right and proper that she, who was there at the beginning, should be there at the end. But he was astonished to see Nesta Serfontein sitting primly on a high-backed chair in a corner of the room. She looked completely at home in her surroundings.

Jack looked at her questioningly.

"It's a small town, Detective Malepo," she smiled. "Hennie was my last surviving relative. I'm here to pay my respects, and if possible, get some answers myself."

Jack gratefully accepted a cup of coffee from Thuli and looked at the people staring up at him expectantly.

"This is a long story, and a tragic one. I imagine you'll think very differently about Hendrik van Tonder when you have heard it, as I did. He was no angel, but more than anything, he loved his family, and he was prepared to do anything to protect them."

Jack decided to play the tape from the beginning. The scene that appeared on the television screen was very different to their interview room at the police station, and for a few moments Jack felt the need to re-orientate himself. The pale green walls and the chairs upholstered in green and pink chintz were a far cry from the stark walls, metal table and plastic chairs he was used to seeing on interview tapes.

"It was August 1927. I was seven years old when I first saw Jakkalsvlei. My mother had died of pneumonia, and we took her body in a wooden coffin to Jakkalsvlei to be buried next to her own mother and father, and two of their children who had died before they had reached adulthood. I remember riding in the cart next to the dominee, with my mother's coffin on the back, strapped on carefully to stop it falling off. My father rode behind on his horse. It is only about twelve kilometres but on that day it seemed like a very long journey, and the dominee didn't say a word until the service began. Then he left in the cart straight after my mother was in the ground. It was only when my father left without me that I realised that he was leaving me there. I never saw him again."

Hennie's voice conjured up a different time and a different way of life, unfamiliar to any of them there, apart from Nesta. They could feel the loneliness of the little boy, and they could understand why he attached himself to his big and handsome cousin for companionship and protection. The people in the room were carried along with Hennie through the good times and the bad, until that fateful day in 1964.

As Hennie told the story of the unfortunate women and children whose bones had, years later, been found in the very house in which they sat, Mma Nyembe began to sob, long harsh sobs that shook her body. At last she had found out exactly what had happened to her friends and the children she had loved. The reality was a hundred times worse than her worst fears.

Jack stopped the tape to allow the old woman to compose herself. Thuli sat close to her grandmother, an arm tightly cradling her frail figure. Katie went off to make her a cup of calming peppermint tea.

They waited for Mma Nyembe to get over the worst of her horror, but she could not be comforted. As the tea finally took effect, Thuli took her upstairs to lie on her bed. She waited with her until she dropped off to sleep. They then watched the rest of the story.

As the tape ended, the whole group sat in silence, each one adjusting their perceptions of the man they had all hated.

"I didn't know," whispered Katie, eventually. "He never said anything to anyone. He must have gone through hell. All my life I have believed that he was an evil man, but I was hating the wrong person. I wish I'd known. I wish I'd been kinder to him."

"I still don't understand why Cobus left him the house," said Patrick. "It sounds as if he hated his cousin, so why leave him the house? And why, knowing what he did, why did he move there?"

"I think it was pure evil revenge on Cobus's part," said Jack. "Hennie never knew that Elsie did not die immediately; that she lived for at least another week or two. And he never knew that the bodies were all bricked up in the laundry. The last time he saw them all, they were lying in the garage. He thought that Cobus had somehow disposed of the bodies, and that they were buried somewhere. Cobus was devious and bitter. He probably hoped that one day Hennie would find the bodies and have to dispose of them himself, or admit some sort of culpability for the crimes. Leaving his cousin the house was a sort of revenge from beyond the grave."

"But why did Hennie then move his family into the house?" repeated Patrick.

"I know the answer to that." It was the first time Nesta had contributed to the conversation. "Hennie was living on a policeman's salary, and we all know what policemen earn. He and Hettie were renting their house, and I suppose it seemed practical to move into the house he had inherited."

"Why did my grandmother agree to move there, though?"

"Well, she didn't know what had happened there. Hennie never told her and Elmarie carried that secret with her to the grave," explained Jack.

"That explains why your grandfather threw me out of the house," said Thuli. "He thought I was the ghost of one of those children, there to haunt him. He must have been frightened to death. Frightened of a little girl! From that day on, every time he saw me, he appeared to be angry. I was probably a constant reminder, taunting him. No wonder he seemed to hate me."

"He probably wanted to tell Rick yesterday, knowing it was about to become public knowledge," said Julie thoughtfully. "He wouldn't have wanted Rick to hear it from anyone but himself. The shock probably caused Rick to have the second stroke."

They spent a long time going over the story in detail, many events in their lives suddenly making sense and taking on a new significance. Eventually, Julie stood up and took charge.

"Katie, you and Patrick should come with me. We have a lot of work to do, and a double funeral to arrange."

"If you're in agreement," said Nesta Serfontein, "I'd like Hennie to be buried on the farm, next to his mother. It would make me very happy if he could find peace there. And you could bury Rick there too. He does have the right to be buried there. He is family."

Katie's natural good manners warred with her horror at the thought. Having just listened with gathering sympathy to the hard and unhappy years Hennie had spent at Jakkalsvlei, she baulked at the thought of taking him back to the place he had escaped from at the first opportunity, to leave him there for all eternity.

"I'm sorry, Auntie, but I just can't do it," Katie said, eventually. "It seems that everything in his life that went wrong has its roots in that place. I think the farm is cursed, and I don't want him to be buried there. Besides, he would have wanted to be buried beside my grandmother and Elmarie."

The service took place three days later. The cemetery was depressing and impersonal – a large dry piece of land at the edge of the town, lined with dusty cypress trees. Most of the graves were untended and covered with weeds, with just the occasional grave decorated with a bunch of faded plastic flowers.

Julie and Katie stood hand in hand beside the open graves, with Patrick standing large and supportive behind them. The holes had been dug next to each other, beside the graves of Hettie and Elmarie. It would be some months before the gravestones would be placed at the head of each grave. There did not appear to be any spare sites in the immediate vicinity, and Thuli wondered where Julie would be buried when the time came.

At last the ordeal was over, and the subdued group started to walk back to their cars.

"Is that where you want to be buried, Auntie Julie?" asked Thuli.

"Dear God, no!" exclaimed Julie. "I hate the thought of being buried. I have already told Katie that I want to be cremated. Besides, I hope never to return to this place again."

Thuli looked at her, confused.

"To this cemetery?" she asked.

"No, has Katie not told you?" she smiled happily. "They have asked me to come and live with them in England, and I have accepted. They have a lovely big house in St Albans, with a separate two-bedroom cottage on the grounds. I will be close to them but still have my independence."

"Oh!" said Thuli sadly. "I'm very pleased for you, but I will miss you terribly."

"And I will certainly miss you. But this way I will get to see my grandchildren grow up."

She smiled across at Katie, who patted her stomach suggestively, smiling happily at Thuli.

"Are you ...?"

"Yes!" exclaimed Katie, her delight mirrored in Patrick's face. "The doctor confirmed it a few days ago. Of course we won't be telling anyone for a while, but you are more like a sister than a friend."

"Well, I certainly can't compete with that," laughed Thuli. "You had just better make sure that the spare bedroom is kept ready, because when that baby arrives, I intend to be there."

Chapter 43

The cemetery at Jakkalsvlei had not changed much since the day in 1927 when Johanna van Tonder was buried. The cypress trees were taller but the farm looked very much as it had then. Only the old farmhouse looked different. It had been unoccupied for twenty-two years, since Oom Jaco had died and Tant Sarie had moved in with Nesta and her family. The roof was gone, and the wood of the stoep had rotted away, leaving the windowless walls between which the chickens foraged for food.

Nesta stood in the very spot she had occupied on the day that Hennie had entered her life. Her memory was of a frightened little boy watching his father ride out of his life. She had hoped for a friend. Instead, she had been subjected to a younger version of her abusive brother.

Cobus had turned out to be the worst kind of role model for the lonely little boy who had lost his parents. Oom Jaco was a humourless man and a hard taskmaster who saw the boy more as a labourer than as a son. Tant Sarie, although she loved her children, was too much in awe of her domineering husband to show either boy any real affection, which Oom Jaco would have probably considered inappropriate. Hennie's childhood had ended the day he arrived on that farm.

Nesta had forgiven Hennie many years ago for trying to rape her when she was a girl. She now felt only pity for the boy who had been betrayed by all the people who should have cared for him. She thought of all the times she had seen him around town over the past fifty years. She had never crossed the street to tell him how she felt. She now bitterly regretted all the missed opportunities.

As she looked across the dry veld, Nesta saw a cloud of red dust which eventually transformed into two cars. Mma Nyembe, Thuli and Jack emerged from one car, while Julie, Katie and Patrick got out of the other.

For Mma Nyembe, this was the second most difficult day of her life. It was the first time she had set foot on Jakkalsvlei since that fateful day, a lifetime ago. She caught her breath at the sight of the vlei with its cool water tumbling over the rocks, surrounded by lush willow trees trailing their slender branches into the water. In her mind's eye, all she could see was the children trying to escape the knobkierrie that was breaking their bones. She could still hear their screams and the sound of Mma Josie's head crashing onto the rock. She looked towards the gravel track, to where the Black Maria had stood, back doors open, as the children and Mma Elsie cowered inside. She recalled with crystal clarity the sound that Mma Josie's body made as Cobus tossed it into the vehicle after them. Her eyes then followed the direction of the rutted track towards Standerton; the direction taken by the vehicle, which had eventually disappeared in a cloud of dust.

She still blamed herself for not doing something, anything, to save them all.

The tears gathered in her eyes and she brushed them away. At least she had found out the truth. That was something to be grateful for.

She heard someone at her side. It was Nesta Serfontein. Nesta took her hand and held it close to her chest for a few moments. Then they walked silently but companionably together towards the people gathered near the little fenced-off cemetery. In the distance, they could hear the two young couples laughing and talking, making plans for the future.

"We are the only ones seeing the ghosts here today," said Nesta with a sad smile, "and when we finally pass, as will surely happen quite soon, these ghosts will finally have their peace."

Epilogue

The two old women sat down under the gazebo that had been erected over the memorial which had been built beside the vlei. The minister stood waiting for everyone to gather, and then the service began.

Agnes Vilikazi and the few remaining relatives of the dead children stood to one side. On the other side was a choir from the local school.

As the minister finished his sermon, a sweet, clear voice rose up from amongst the children gathered around the memorial. It was joined by the rest of the choir in sweet harmony. It was a fitting farewell to the lost children, to Elsie, and to Josie, the loving teacher who had given her life trying to protect them all. Tears flowed freely; there was no one who remained unaffected by the moment. Even the minister found himself wiping his tears away with his spotless white handkerchief.

The song ended and silence fell. Everyone was wrapped in their own private thoughts.

After several minutes, Nesta Serfontein leaned across to Anna Nyembe and lightly touched her arm, nodding her head towards the west, where the approaching dusk had turned the sky into an artist's dreamscape. The colours ranged from pale yellow to the deepest lilac.

The sun was setting over Jakkalsvlei. It was time to put the ghosts to rest.

Charmaine Stewart

Charmaine Stewert was born and raised in the Old Transvaal, and moved to Sandton in the late 1960's. She lived the life of a model citizen for the first 20 years of her adult life, working hard and raising her three children. She returned to university full time as a 'mature' student and obtained a B.Comm degree in 1985. Charmaine's passions have always been travelling, reading and writing.

When she reached her forties, Charmaine felt that life was passing her by and she craved adventure. She and her husband moved to Namibia where they built and ran the Langholm Hotel for 10 years while exploring the country.

They sold the hotel after a decade of hard work and decided to spend the next ten years in England. They fondly refer to this period as their 'gap decade'. They both worked, and used England as a base from which to explore the UK and Europe, with a trip along the west coast of the States and Canada.

While in England, Charmaine started writing again, partly to fill those long cold nights, and she has thoroughly enjoyed getting back into it. Her writing is based partly on the tales told by her parents and their friends, and partly from memories from her childhood.

Charmaine and her husband are now back in Namibia where she still finds time to write and hopes to follow up The Innocent Bones with another story featuring Jack Malepo soon.